MW01615897

Murder
Is Only Skin Deep

Yvonne Deitz
Vikki Moormann
Susan Schreiber

PublishAmerica
Baltimore

ISBN: 1-4241-4843-X
PUBLISHED BY PUBLISHAMERICA, LLLP
www.publishamerica.com
Baltimore

Printed in the United States of America

Acknowledgments

Ed Campbell for help with police procedurals

Dr. Robert West for help with forensics

Kathie Adkinson for reading
and making editing suggestions

Pam Alliano for editing suggestions

Todd Snyder for help with graphic design and technical assistance

Dr. and Mrs. Richard Barclay for technical assistance,
encouragement, and proofreading

Don Moormann for his support

David Schreiber for being a morale booster and reader

This book is dedicated to all our former students who worked so hard to write for us; we now understand how difficult it was to write with clarity, precision, and accuracy.

Chapter 1
Thrash the Trash

The whirring sound of the sprinkler droned lazily in the distance as Jean opened the French doors to the deck and back yard. Holding her coffee mug, she sank into one of the deck chairs and surveyed the peaceful morning scene before her. The scent of freshly mowed grass and the soft, sweet air came close to hypnotizing her. Mt. Spokane shimmered hazily in the distance as it stood guard over the Spokane Valley, the Eastern Washington community that she had called home for almost thirty years. Lacy leaves of the red maple whispered softly overhead and cast dappled shadows on the deck while the Shasta daisies along the fence seemed to nod happily in the sunshine. "Mmmm," she thought languidly, "I seem to have a case of Summer Syndrome—be lazy; be useless; be happy." Raking her hands through her short, salt and pepper hair, Jean made a real attempt at moving out of the chair and onto the agenda she had planned for the morning.

"The first order of business must be to put dust on the roses," she reminded herself firmly. "Then the geraniums in the planters must be dead-headed and the weeds in the perennial bed attacked, but maybe before I do that, I'll run upstairs and sneak a quick peek at my e-mail. Surely there must be news of someone." Sally, her old teaching buddy, was supposed to be home from New York. "She knows I'm dying to hear about her trip. Plus, we do need to meet with Eileen very soon to rehash the notes for Chapter 8." Jean smiled nostalgically as she thought of their school days and the joy she had when teaching, but shook off the past quickly and grinned in excitement about the book she and Sally were trying to write.

The computer warmed up slowly, and Jean continued to gaze out the upstairs window. Indeed the roses and the weeds were still waiting for her tender care. "I'm coming, I'm coming," she promised quietly to herself as she watched her fat, black cat, Mrs. Robinson, lounging in the sun. "Maybe cats have the right idea after all," she thought bemusedly to herself. "Weeding is probably not on their list of priorities ever."

Internet service, at least, was obliging and on task this morning. After she heard the familiar "You've got mail" singing to her, Jean pulled up several messages. Three advertisements: lower interest rates, cut rate prescriptions, and a special deal for magazine subscriptions all received a quick "Delete," but a message from her friend Beth Milner in Kalispell demanded an immediate "Open."

Subject: Divorce!
Date: 7/22/00 4:15 PM Pacific Standard Time
From: BMilner@my180.net
To: JSmiley@aol.com

Dear Jean,
Imagine my surprise when I scrolled through the recycle bin of my computer (trying to find a copy of my resume that somehow has evaporated) and found a letter to Max promising undying love. The crux of the letter seemed to imply that said "undying love" was an old, but brightly burning one and longed for a meeting very soon. Signed only with a "C", the return address read CWIK@aol.com. Can you imagine????

Lover boy, of course, pled total innocence and raged AT ME for being a snoop. I, on the other hand, remained calm, cool, and

8

collected (NOT) as I railed at him for his Nixon stupidity at NOT DESTROYING THE EVIDENCE. What the hell was he starting, a Casanova Collection? Believe me, the air was blue and the recriminations almost unendurable. As I (calmly, once again) sobbed and beat my breast, Romeo stormed out the door (with nary a pair of undies) vowing that "maybe, just maybe, I can find some peace and quiet in Missoula."

I declare, Jean, I am at sixes and sevens, if not sixties and seventies. After thirty years of marriage, one really thinks she has the inside track. For two weeks I have been brooding in solitude. Even though, I still wonder how I could have been so thickheaded and blind. I have thought and thought about dear Juliet and how this smoldering "undying love" didn't even leave one trace of smoke. The children, of course, are frantic and puzzled and furious. You and I have been friends for so long, and you know I have always admired your keen insight and ability to get to the heart of the matter. Please! Can you help by maybe going to Missoula and seeing if you can learn anything?

Beth

Jean stared blankly at the screen. How on earth could this be? Beth and Max Milner had not only been married for thirty years, but had been an item for eight years before that.

She remembered the first time they went to the Missoula High School prom—the eight of them had gone together, stuffed into Max's father's station wagon. The giggly, gorgeous girls in their bouffant dresses had tried so hard to be sophisticated. Beth in pale blue; Mary Carol in shimmering silver; Crystal in black; and she in lavender; each girl sure that she could honestly answer the question, "Who is the fairest of them all?" She remembered the boys had worked hard at being nonchalant, but even good old Max was a tad nervous, especially when it came to posing for pictures. But that was long, long ago, Jean chided herself sternly—plenty of water under the bridge since then: college, weddings, children, reunions, and even death. "Gracious, I can't sit here all morning mooning about the past," Jean scolded herself.

What on earth could have possessed Max? Midlife crises? Boredom? A roving eye that he had kept well hidden? Maybe someone at work had pursued him, but that would have been at least a year ago. Max had been retired now for almost a year and a half.

"There certainly does not appear to be an answer from this perch," Jean decided. "Should I fly off to Missoula and snoop about, or should I tend to my garden and lollygag in the sunshine?" Almost before she could even begin to weigh the pros and cons, her hands were on the computer keyboard, punching resolutely on the reply button.

Subject: Divorce
Date: 7/23/00 10:16 AM Pacific Standard Time
From: JSmiley@aol.com
To: BMilner@my180.net

Beth Dear,

I am astonished to hear your unhappy news and can only begin to imagine your dismay, probably much stronger than dismay——devastation would be more likely. Surely you have searched your memory bank for clues, past and present?

Anyway what good would that do at this point? Max seems to have flown the coop, and the question is does he want to continue on the midlife flight or return to his senses. I guess you can't determine this until you at least have a chance to speak with him. Have you any idea where he is in Missoula? Why not check with Mary Carol yourself?

On the other hand, there is certainly no reason why I can't help you with a little undercover work. The garden will wait, and it's the perfect time of year for a little trip. I'll talk to MC this morning and see if she's game for a visitor. It will take a bit of time to tie up a few loose ends here, but will try to be on the road by Thursday morning. I'll be in touch by the beginning of next week. In the meantime, wrack your brain and maybe some additional computer files, and by Jove, we will get to the bottom of this. Chin up!

Jean

The lassitude that had threatened Jean earlier that morning seemed to disappear like dust after a rainstorm. A quick call to Missoula revealed that Mary Carol must have been working at Powell and Powell, Attorneys at Law. Jean could never get her friend and sister-in-law's part-time schedule firmly in mind. Nevertheless, she left a voice mail message explaining that she needed to get out of Dodge and inquiring if there were room at the corral. Smiling at her own feeble wit, she asked Mary Carol to call her after work to confirm the plan which involved arrival on the coming Thursday. Somehow she itched to get this sleuthing underway. "Must be just what the doctor ordered," she thought bemusedly. "Old friends are infinitely more important that aphids and weeds."

After hand-watering her African Violets, she called John Houck, her next door neighbor, and coerced him into watering her lawn for a few days while she was gone. "You can easily walk next door when you move your hose," she pleaded. "And I promise to bake you an apple pie as soon as I get back." It took only a few minutes to throw her clothes into a suitcase and gather up Mrs. Robinson's spare litter box, carrier, and several cans of food. By mid-afternoon, everything seemed to be in place: library books returned, bills paid, even one flowerbed was conquered.

By four o'clock the porch swing and a glass of Chardonnay called her name. Jean settled in to review old times once again and ponder the wayward actions of Mr. Max. "He has always been a good-looking fellow," she mused. Biking, hiking, outdoor activities had kept him vital and in good shape. Beth, on the other hand, had preferred to stay at home to keep the home fires burning. Come to think of it, she pretty much cut the wood and stoked the fire. When the kids were small, she stayed and tended the home front while Max skied, or shot the rapids, or went deep-sea fishing. "I wonder, though, about Beth's reference to her resume. Wouldn't retirement time be the perfect chance for them to travel and enjoy some time together? Why a resume and a job now? Was this maybe a threat to..." The phone rang shrilly, not only interrupting Jean's reverie, but also scaring Mrs. Robinson plum off the swing and onto the porch steps.

Jean answered on the third ring to hear a familiar voice drawling on the other end. "Well, pardner, this is Mary Carol at the old corral. The stalls are crying for company, so hitch up Old Bessie and get yourself on over here."

"Oh, Mary Carol, I was sure you'd have me. Somehow I just have a yen to travel and see some old friends. Must be retirement catching up with me, I guess. August is coming, and I have no pencils to sharpen, no bulletin boards to create, and no lessons to prepare for the first time in thirty-three years. Just don't know what to do with myself, I guess."

"I have to go in and help take a deposition Friday morning, and then I am through until Tuesday, so we can spend a long weekend together. Can you think of anyone you'd like to see while you're here?"

"Just seeing you will be great," Jean replied sincerely, "but you know, it might be fun to rustle up some of the old gang on Saturday or Sunday and see how the senior years are treating all of us. Wouldn't have to be anything spectacular, maybe a picnic. What do you think?"

"Sounds good to me. You know that even with old friends so close by, not many of us take the time to stay in touch. As usual it takes a friendly nudge from someone 'down the road.' What time do you think you'll get here tomorrow?"

"I'd think about 5:00 or 5:30," Jean calculated quickly. "If you'll chill a bottle of Chardonnay, I'll bring some Pinot Noir for you."

"OK, Kiddo, I'm looking forward to seeing you."

"Mary Carol, Mrs. Robinson won't be any trouble, will she?"

"She never has been before, Jean. Might be a good time to check on the mouse population anyway. See you tomorrow in time for a cocktail."

"Thanks, Mary Carol. See you tomorrow then. Bye."

Chapter 2
Journey Through Time

As Jean pulled her car onto Interstate 90 heading toward Missoula, she couldn't help but wonder what she was getting herself into. After all, she was just a retired English teacher. Granted she had a vivid imagination and adored reading murder mysteries, but really…finding out who Max was having an affair with seemed a little beyond her ken. It seemed more a problem that a trained investigator could solve. Maybe she should talk to her neighbor, John Houck, when she got home. After all, he had just retired from the Spokane Police Department last spring after thirty-one years on the force. He might be much more adept at facing the arduous task of discovering the identity of the infamous "C" of e-mail fame. Oh well, she had promised Beth, and she would keep her promise.

She glanced down at her favorite feline, settling on her blanket on the front seat. Mrs. Robinson really traveled quite well and only occasionally had to be put into the cat carrier when she became a little cantankerous. Jean enjoyed her company as she drove, and Mrs. Robinson would "chat" with her as the miles flashed by.

She turned on her favorite tape, the sound track to *Titanic* and let her mind wander freely as she headed toward the Idaho state line and then Coeur d'Alene. Jean was pleased to see the deep blue sky and bright sun. It gave her a sense of serenity and hope.

As she passed through Coeur d'Alene, she remembered how her high school friends Crystal and Bill Pemberton used to love to come from Missoula to the Coeur d'Alene Resort for a week or two every year. Bill loved to go fly fishing in some of the surrounding rivers while Crystal spent her time browsing in the art galleries and doing some heavy duty shopping. Jean reflected that perhaps at times Bill loved fly fishing more than he seemed to love Crystal, his wife of many years.

"Well, at times who wouldn't!" she snorted to herself.

Mrs. Robinson resettled her not so trim, sleek, black body and meowed in agreement.

Thinking of Bill and Crystal brought sadness to her heart. They all missed Bill so much. Even though she was devout in her faith in God, Jean still could not understand how God had allowed Bill to develop Alzheimer 's disease. Bill gave so much to the community and to his friends. He supported many local charitable foundations, volunteered his time at the hospital, and was always willing to help out a friend, no matter what. Everyone who knew him enjoyed spending time with him! Then over time he had become a withdrawn, almost sullen man.

There had been hope for a while. Crystal had talked to Robert Sheffield, Bill's doctor and their friend from high school, and they had decided to try him on a new, rather experimental drug. Within months Crystal had written that Bill seemed to be improving and that he was almost himself again. He was doing so well that he had been able to go fishing by himself. In fact, he had been begging Crystal to let him go fly-fishing at his favorite spot in the Flathead Valley near Whitefish, Montana. Since the doctor hadn't been able to give any guarantees as to how long into the future this supposed recovery would last, Crystal had finally relented and told him yes, that now was probably a good time to go.

Unfortunately, she had been unable to go with him. Oh, how she must regret not going with him that last time! How she must wish she had not had that art show that week, even though some of her young protégés were the focal point of the show! With Crystal's help Bill had planned the trip carefully. He planned to drive up to Whitefish and stay at their favorite bed and breakfast. Then for two days he would spend his time fishing the south fork of the Flathead River but would return to the B and B well before dark. Crystal had told Jean he had been so excited he had purchased a new rod and flies to catch those elusive trout. Because Crystal was still quite worried about him, they had agreed that she would call each evening at 9:00. She could surreptitiously check on his well being, and he could tell her of his day.

The night of his arrival, Bill was so excited when he talked to Crystal on the phone he could hardly contain himself. The drive up had been exhilarating. He had seen some deer and even, he thought, an elk. He believed the weather would be perfect for early summer fishing.

The next night when Crystal tried to call, there had been no answer in Bill's room. She thought perhaps he was late getting back from dinner and would call her upon his return. When once again there was no response, she had called and talked to the owners of the B and B. They told her they had not seen Bill since he left that morning. She asked if they would check his room, which they did. The husband even looked out back to see if Bill's car were there. It wasn't. Crystal had panicked.

She asked the owners for the number of the local police. She then called the police and voiced her concerns. They informed her rather curtly that it was much too soon to declare a person missing. They went so far as to tell her he probably would get over it (whatever "it" was) and come home when he was ready. She decided to wait one more day. If she had heard nothing by dinnertime the next day, she would drive up there herself.

Crystal had said that she was a basket case that night. Every little sound would jerk her awake in the hopes it was Bill coming into the house to tell her about the lousy fishing and what a disaster the whole trip had been. She had not left the house the entire day, hoping against hope that the phone would ring, and it would be Bill laughing about what had happened to him.

Around 4:30 that afternoon, she had started gathering a few things together for a trip to Flathead Valley. She had asked Mary

Carol, who lived next door, to come over for last minute instructions for the mail and newspapers. As they were speaking, the front door bell rang. Crystal raced to the door. Standing with his hat in hand was Lt. Fred Williamson of the Montana State Police. It was his sad duty, he said, to inform her of her husband's drowning in the Flathead River. Another fisherman had discovered Bill's body that morning. It looked as if he had slipped, been pulled under from the weight of the water in his waders, and had been unable to get up again; eventually he had drowned in the swift-running river. Crystal had fainted dead away. Mary Carol had overheard the conversation and rushed to her aid. Mary Carol had assured Fred she would get someone to go to Whitefish that evening. She and Crystal would be there sometime the next day.

Mary Carol had always had a tender heart, and, as a result, she was always ready to offer help whenever it was needed. This time was no exception. She had taken charge and called Jean first, then Bill's doctor Robert and his wife Caren, who lived in Missoula, and finally Max and Beth in Kalispell to let them know what had happened. Robert, as usual, wasn't home, but Caren said she would call him on his pager at the hospital. He was unable to call back until 10:00 that evening. Max, however, had been ever so gracious and had agreed to drive to Whitefish immediately. Max had been on his way to Missoula anyway for a business meeting, which he assured her he could delay. He would speak with the Whitefish police and do whatever he could. Mary Carol assured him that she and Crystal would be there the next morning and gave him the number of the motel where they could be reached. Mary Carol had wondered what she would do without him.

When Mary Carol had called Jean again the next morning from Whitefish to explain what had transpired, she had sounded emotionally and physically drained. When Jean talked to Crystal, she could only moan, "Why did I let him go? WHY?" Jean could certainly understand her remorse, but she could also understand why Crystal had let him go.

Jean reminded Crystal, "Remember Bill died doing what he loved most. In fact, he was probably in heaven right now, checking out the new fly fishing supplies and best rivers." Crystal had laughed weakly in agreement.

Thinking of Bill made Jean think of the last time the gang from high school had been together. They had attended two funerals in two years for two of their own group, a sobering reminder of their own mortality. First Johnny, Jean's own dear twin brother and husband to Mary Carol, had died in a horrible head-on collision caused by an insane drunk driver and then Bill! Not one of them had ever expected to be attending the funeral of one of the gang so soon after Johnny's death the previous fall.

At Bill's funeral Crystal had been an emotional wreck, even worse than Mary Carol had been when she was widowed by Johnny's death. Jean had never seen Crystal in such a state. Max had spent a lot of time trying to offer her solace as all of them had, but Max had been the only one who seemed to be able to penetrate her miasma of sorrow. He was the only one to whom Crystal seemed to listen.

As Jean became more focused on the road, she realized she had already crossed over Lookout Pass and was on her way toward St. Regis, Montana. Maybe she would stop there for something to drink. She let Mrs. Robinson know they would be stopping for a little bit. Maybe she could even take the cat for a short walk on her leash before they got back on the road. Mrs. Robinson loved the attention she attracted when she went for her walks. Yes, that was a good idea. After all, Mary Carol wasn't expecting her until 5:30 or so.

Jean thought about Mary Carol and smiled. She was such a dear person. No wonder Jean's twin brother Johnny had adored her. They had been married for over thirty years when Johnny had died a year ago last September. Jean still missed her brother and had really tried hard to keep a close friendship with Mary Carol. It bothered Jean that Mary Carol had seemed so distant over the past few months. They used to keep in touch on a fairly regular basis, but lately, Mary Carol was never home when Jean called, and Mary Carol didn't seem to call Jean very often the way she had before. Well, it certainly was time to renew their friendship.

After ordering lemonade at the restaurant in St. Regis, Jean's thoughts drifted. Again, she thought of Bill. She remembered yet

18

another time the whole group had been together. It had been their fortieth class reunion at Missoula High School. In fact, it was just two years ago last August. What a wonderful time they had all had!

Caren and Robert, whose strange relationship was marked by disagreement, had actually stopped arguing for those three days and had seemed almost pleasant toward each other. Caren had looked dramatic in a gold lame designer gown she wore to the dinner, and, of course, Robert looked like the doctor he was in his white dinner jacket.

Beth and Max had been there, too. Beth, as usual, had shown her less than fashionable taste in wearing a rather dowdy-looking beige dress for the formal dinner. It had totally washed her out. And, of course, her dishwater blonde hair looked as if it needed a firm hand. It certainly was a good thing she was such a competent, pleasant person to be around. Max, as usual, was his charming, handsome self. Jean reflected he had been more charming than ever. He had danced with all of the ladies. In fact, he had danced with that other striking brunette at the dinner. What was her name? HMMMM?

Jean's brother had been there with Mary Carol, and Johnny had looked as debonair as ever. (Jean certainly knew who of the fraternal twins had gotten the attractive gene...and it wasn't she!) His laughter had carried across the crowded dance floor, and whenever Jean had heard it, she smiled, too. In fact, she smiled now when she remembered. No matter how much Johnny had tried to help Mary Carol with her choice of clothing or hairstyle, she always looked like a small disaster in the making with a run in her hose or her slip showing a bit.

And then there were Crystal and Bill. What a loving couple! Even though Bill had just recently been diagnosed with Alzheimer's, there were only a few telltale clues for someone who was really looking to know something was wrong. He looked as physically fit as always and had that tan he always got in the summer from spending days (weeks if you heard Crystal tell the story) in the rivers of Idaho and Montana fly fishing. Crystal was her usual stunning self with her glorious, thick, black hair cascading down around white, shapely shoulders. And that diamond necklace she was wearing! It could have fed a third world country for at least six months. Bill was very proud of her and the necklace he had just given her. Who would have thought that in just a little under two years he would be gone?

Jean thought sadly about her own solitary status for one brief moment and then decided that she had managed quite well through the years, thank you very much!

Well, enough of this dreaming. She walked resolutely to her car, attached Mrs. Robinson's leash to her collar, and took her for a short walk. When her curious feline decided to chase after a scurrying chipmunk, Jean hauled her back and looked at her watch. She had to get back on the road. She figured she had about two hours left to drive, and she lured Mrs. Robinson into her cat carrier with a treat for the remainder of the trip.

As the miles flew by, Jean once again thought about her reason for going to Missoula. How was she going to help Beth determine what was really going on with Max? Was there a chance Beth and Max could be reconciled? Who was this "C" person who had confessed undying love? How long had the affair really been going on? From what Beth said, it sounded like a while. Well, she would do her best to learn the identity of "C" and find out how Max really felt about Beth. Who could "C" be? She only knew Crystal and Caren. Could it be one of them? No, certainly not Crystal; she was still too devastated by the loss of Bill. Caren? Well, maybe. Someone else? She would just have to ask some subtle questions and see what happened.

Chapter 3
Chardonnay, and Who Is "C"?

Mrs. Robinson emitted a plaintive "Meow!", and Jean responded with, "Just a few more miles, Sweetie. We're almost there." She glanced at her watch. "About thirty minutes or so, and we'll be stretching our legs at your Aunt Mary Carol's. In fact, there's the exit right ahead." With that, Jean began signaling for a right turn off the Interstate.

After maneuvering through several streets and traffic, Jean and Mrs. Robinson were winding their way into the gracious, older residential area around the University of Montana. Jean loved this part of town with the tall, old trees arching over the streets like a cathedral ceiling; the old houses with their lawns, flower gardens, trees, and shrubs displayed the characters of their owners through the years.

"Right on time!" she announced as she pulled up in front of a white, two-story, brick-trimmed home. Jean noted the well-manicured lawn and rose bushes in front and thought briefly about her own roses at home, which would still be waiting for her attention. "Oh, well…" Her watch showed 5:00 o'clock "I told Mary Carol 5:00 or 5:30, and here we are! Be right back to get you, Mrs. R., but first we need to make sure we can get in."

Jean shut off the ignition, opened her car door, and emerged, stretching. "Hooee! It feels good to stand up." She walked to the front door and rang the bell, just in case Mary Carol might be home, and hearing no sound, reached for the key hidden inside the fake rock next to the steps hoping that Mary Carol still kept it there. She was in luck, and after opening the door, she looked around to make sure no one saw her replace the "rock" to its usual place and went back to the car for Mrs. Robinson and her clothes.

As she entered the house with her garment bag and small travel case, the phone was ringing. Jean draped the garment bag over the back of a nearby chair and dropped her travel bag to the floor. "Hello," she said rather breathlessly.

"Carol?" asked a masculine voice on the other end.

"No, this is her sister-in-law. Mary Carol should be home in just a few minutes. May I take a message?" The receiver on the other end clicked, and then it was silent.

"Hello...Hello! That's strange. I never knew anyone who ever called Mary Carol by her middle name before. And then to just hang up! That seems rude. I hope she's not getting some kind of crank calls or being bothered by a masher of some sort," she thought as she returned to the car for Mrs. Robinson.

Just as Jean was setting Mrs. Robinson's cat carrier down on the floor, she heard the sound of the garage door opening, and within a minute the two ladies were greeting each other with happy shrieks and hugs.

"I'm so glad you came! You look wonderful, Jean."

"I look good—what about you? I've never seen you look so terrific!" exclaimed Jean. "Turn around, and let me get a good look at you. What have you done to yourself? You look ten years younger! What is your secret?" She smiled at her sister-in-law and examined her from every angle. Mary Carol did, indeed, look very good. She was wearing a trim, beige, silk suit, her short-cropped auburn hair had no trace of the usual gray, her skin was milky and translucent, and she was wearing a hint of make-up, something she had not done since Johnny died.

"No real secret. A friend of mine at the office and I have been going to Weight-Watchers for a few months now; we've been walking during our lunch hours, and then we decided to have a beauty consultation after her sister got involved in selling a new line of cosmetics. It's been a lot of fun. That's all, but thanks, I'm glad you approve." Mary Carol's blue-green eyes sparkled happily.

For one uneasy second the thought "Carol = C" flashed into Jean's mind, but she immediately dismissed it.

"Oh, here, let me help you take your things up to the guest room, and Mrs. Robinson can have the screened back porch to roam again." She reached down to let the cat out of her cage and was immediately rewarded with Mrs. Robinson's loud purring and rubbing against her legs. Giving a friendly scratch on the top of Mrs. Robinson's black head, she crooned, "What nice, silky ears you have, Mrs. R."

Mary Carol turned to Jean. "Why don't you get settled in your usual spot, hang your clothes in the closet, and go ahead and put your personal items in your bathroom—the top drawer is empty for you—and I'll get our black, furry friend here settled in her usual place. Then come on down to the living room, and I'll bring us a little snack while we catch up and then think about dinner. I have a bottle of chardonnay chilling in the fridge and some Brie and crackers to tide us over. I thought for your first night here we could celebrate with dinner out. My treat."

"No, no! We're camping out at your place. Let this be my treat," protested Jean.

"Oh, oh, here we go again. Tell you what. We'll flip a coin, and that will decide it once and for all. No argument."

"Okay. Okay, that sounds fair enough. Oh, I almost forgot. I have a bottle of Pinot Noir under the front seat for you. Remember I promised to bring that for you. Where would you like me to put it?"

"Just put it in the wine rack on the kitchen counter."

"Okay. Sounds good. I'll move my car off the street then, too. I presume you would like it on the right side of the driveway, or have you rearranged things in the garage since the last time I was here?"

"Nope, just put your car in the usual spot."

"Okay. Be right back."

As she maneuvered her Honda into Mary Carol's driveway, Jean thought about the change in her sister-in-law's appearance. This once rather frumpy lady was now anything but that. It wasn't just outward either. There was a kind of inner glow about her, and it was very becoming. "I wonder…"

Minutes later Jean had sunk into the velvety olive cushions of the love seat angled next to the couch where Mary Carol sat with her shoes on the floor and her feet tucked under her. They reached in turn for the silver cheese spreader, herbed Brie and buttery crackers on the small tray placed on the end table between them as they sipped their wine and chatted easily.

"Oh, I almost forgot," Jean said suddenly. "The phone was ringing when I first let myself into the house. I thought it might be you calling to see if I were here, so I answered it. Some man just said, 'Carol?' and I told him, no, it was her sister-in-law, and could I take a message, and he just hung up. Wasn't that strange?"

An indefinable look crossed Mary Carol's face as she answered slowly, "Yes, yes, it is rather strange. Well, um…" she stammered. "Here, let me give you a little more chardonnay."

At that moment the phone rang, Mary Carol jumped, and her hand brushed against Jean's glass, tipping it over and spilling the contents over the glass-topped table on which it had been sitting.

"Oh, no! Did I spill any on you? Let me get something to wipe that up."

"Mary Carol, it's fine. Look, the glass did not have much left in it, and it just spilled on the top of the table. No harm done to anything. You'd better get the phone, though, before the caller hangs up. It might be the person who called earlier. I'll get a paper towel from the kitchen and take care of this." Jean picked up the overturned glass and hurried into the kitchen.

Just as she returned with a paper towel and the dishcloth, which had been hanging over the kitchen sink, Jean heard Mary Carol speaking into the phone.

"I can't talk to you right now. Jean is here. Just got in from Spokane, and we were having a glass of wine together. Talk to you soon, though, as soon as possible." She was almost whispering, and she had her back to the kitchen door.

"That wouldn't be some secret admirer, would it?" teased Jean gently.

Mary Carol's face turned crimson and she avoided Jean's eyes as she said rather stiffly, "No, it wasn't anything like that."

"I was only kidding, Mary Carol. I know how you felt about Johnny, and when you reach the point that you are able to be open to a new relationship, I will just be happy for you, and I'm sure many other people will be, too."

Mary Carol smiled at her sister-in-law. "Thanks. That means a lot to me." Her face relaxed, and she added, "That was Max."

Chapter 4
Plan a Picnic and Invite the C's

Jean was momentarily taken aback when she heard that Max was the caller. "Max? Is he here in Missoula now?" she asked, pretending she knew nothing about his flight from Beth and their home in Kalispell.

"Yes, he is here now, and he has been for two weeks," Mary Carol responded seriously. "I hate to be the bearer of bad news, but apparently he and Beth have had some kind of problems, and Max came to me asking for help in finding a good divorce lawyer. He thought I might have some knowledge about that sort of thing because my bosses handle a lot of divorce cases."

"The problems must be pretty serious then," Jean commented, and then added carefully, "Did he give you any clues about the problems?"

"No, not really, but for some reason he seems to think that Beth just might be trying to get as much from him as she can get if things actually come to a head and end in divorce, and he wants to protect his assets. Max has always been one to help out his friends when they have been in need, so I've been checking into this matter with my bosses. I'd like to help him if I can."

Mary Carol stood up suddenly. "Look here! You did not drive all this way to listen to people's problems. Let's go out and get a nice dinner, plan our get-together, and make a list of people to call tomorrow and get things rolling!"

"Sounds good to me. Where shall we go, and when shall we flip a coin to see who's treating whom?"

"If you're in the mood for Italian cuisine, I thought we might go to the Waterfront Pasta House. I could even be persuaded to break my diet for this occasion and have at least a scoop of their sinfully rich ice cream for dessert. They make their own, and it is good!"

"That sounds good to me; let's go there!"

"Now for the coin!" Jean went up to the guest bedroom to get her purse and was back in the living room before either of them could say, "Mrs. Robinson." She fished a quarter out of the zippered coin section of her small organizer handbag. "You call it. Heads or tails?"

"Heads."

With one deft flip of the quarter, Jean held out her hand with the quarter in her palm and announced triumphantly, "Tails! I win, and I get to treat you this time!"

"Okay, but remember that next time it will be my treat, and no ifs, ands, or buts about it. I'm going to call ahead and see if we can get a table on the deck, so we can look at the river. Does that sound good or what?"

"Italian food, homemade ice cream, eating outside with a view of the river and with my favorite sister-in-law—that sounds like a little slice of heaven to me!" Jean gave Mary Carol a quick hug. "I think I'll give Mrs. Robinson a helping of her favorite canned cat food before we go so that she won't be too jealous."

Jean disappeared to the back porch to gather up the cat's dish and a small can of food from the bag of cat supplies she had brought with her while Mary Carol picked up the phone to check about getting a table on the deck.

An hour later the two ladies were sitting contentedly at a small table overlooking the Clark Fork River eating their salads and sipping white Zinfandel.

"Okay, Jean, who would you especially like to see while you are here? Let's make our guest list."

Jean thought, "Whoever the infamous 'C' might be is a must," and then said aloud, "I haven't seen any of the high school gang since Bill's funeral. Why don't we start with Caren and Robert? I'd like to know how they are and see if they are getting along any better or if they are still picking at each other the way they used to so often. They can be pretty entertaining sometimes." Jean grinned impishly. Then she added more seriously, "Although, I think we're beginning to learn that life's too short to waste energy on small annoyances."

"True," replied Mary Carol, "so we'll start with Robert and Caren and hope they are appreciating each other's positive qualities more. Who else?"

The waiter's bringing their seafood pasta, whisking away their empty salad plates, and refilling their water glasses interrupted them.

After lifting a forkful of food to her mouth, Jean gave a contented sigh. "Mmmm, this is good." The two women spent the next few minutes in relative silence as they enjoyed their meal.

Jean pushed her empty plate aside and stated, "Okay, back to our guest list. I know that Crystal is pretty involved with her foundation for supporting new artists, but I would think she'd be happy to see old friends on a much happier occasion than the last time we were all together, and I'd like to see her again, too. Even though she lives right next door to you, you don't see her or talk to her that much either, from what you've told me."

"That's true. We've both been involved in our own lives, and our paths just don't cross that often. Unless we make a special effort to get together, we simply do not see much of each other. So yes, we'll put Crystal down for sure." Then she added, "What about Max? I'm not sure about how he will feel around old friends without Beth, but it just may be what he needs right now—being with friends."

"You're right about that, M.C. Let's invite Max." Jean was glad that Mary Carol was making things so easy for her by suggesting they invite Max. It would give her an opportunity to observe him around the two "C's" that they knew before she returned home to write down

28

anything she might learn and report back to Beth. At the same time, she was struck with the great empathy Mary Carol was showing toward Max with no words spoken on her part about any kind of pain that Beth might be feeling about the difficulties the couple had been experiencing. Jean wondered if Mary Carol had any inkling about what kinds of problems those might be, and again the uncomfortable thought entered her mind about the mysterious caller who had hung up after asking, "Carol?"

"Okay, Jean. Now all we need to do is set a time for our little gathering and firm it up. You suggested a picnic. That would be very easy, especially if each person would like to contribute a little food, and we can have it in my back yard. The weather has been excellent for outdoor activities, and it's not expected to change in the next few days. What about a day and a time?"

Jean thought quickly, "How about Sunday afternoon? That seems like a good day for a picnic, don't you think? Those who go to church can go in the morning and then have the rest of the day for R and R." She also added to herself, "That way Max and his interactions with the C's will be fresh in my mind before I go home on Tuesday."

"Sunday it is. How does two o'clock sound to you?"

"Perfect. Now what about you, M.C.? Is there anyone else you would like to invite?"

Mary Carol looked down at her plate thoughtfully then looked up and answered, "No, right now I think this guest list is just right."

The rest of the evening went by quickly as the two women enjoyed their food and each other's company. By the time they were finishing their ice cream, the patio lights were on, and they were both feeling comfortably full and a little drowsy.

Mary Carol covered a yawn with her hand and announced, "I hate to end this evening, but we do have three more days to chit chat to our hearts' content, and we need to save some energy to do some serious shopping at the mall! Besides, I have to go to work tomorrow morning."

"I agree. I think it's time to head back to the corral and hit the hay," Jean agreed as she, too, stifled a yawn.

Chapter 5
Dial "2" for "C"

A constant patting of her left cheek brought Jean back to consciousness after a good night's sleep. She realized that Mrs. Robinson had been let upstairs and was now trying to get her attention. That cat! She could be adorable, and then again, she could be a royal pest. She persisted in patting Jean's cheek until she finally groaned and put her arms around the friendly feline. Jean was sure Mrs. Robinson's purring could be heard all the way downstairs. As Jean lay there, enjoying the warm summer morning, she heard Mary Carol downstairs in the kitchen. She thought she had best get up and greet Mary Carol before she left for work. At least she only had to work half a day today, and then they could have the next three and a half days together.

As she showered and dressed, she thought of the things she had to accomplish during the day. First of all, after breakfast she had to start making calls to Caren and Robert, Crystal, and then Max. In her sleuthing mode, she decided to find out who had talked to Max lately to see whom he had been in contact with since moving to Missoula and if anyone had his phone number even though Jean had already gotten it from Mary Carol. If she could reach everyone this morning, then she could have the afternoon free to explore the town and see if any changes had been made.

Entering the kitchen, Jean was surprised to see Mary Carol in a mint green, silky jogging outfit that really complimented her ivory skin, which had a healthy, rosy glow to it this morning. When she commented on it, Mary Carol replied, "Oh, three to four times a week I try to walk at least two miles in the morning before leaving for work." Jean was quite impressed and wondered what had brought about this change in attitude on Mary Carol's part. Whatever it was, it seemed very good for her.

As Mary Carol finished her yogurt and banana, Jean got the box of cereal from the cupboard. She was just putting bread in the toaster when Mary Carol leaped up and exclaimed she had better get going or she would be late for work. Jean was sorry they hadn't had more time to chat, but Mary Carol had never seemed to be a morning person before. Maybe that still held true, even if she got up early three to four times a week to walk. Go figure...

After Mary Carol left for the law office where she worked as a receptionist/secretary, Jean thought she had better call Caren and Robert early. She never knew what Caren's schedule was since she worked at the hospital only three days a week now. Jean remembered when Robert had first opened his practice in Missoula, Caren had been his nurse. That working relationship, however, did not last long. They might love each other, but they had an unusual relationship that seemed to thrive on argument. The patients finally started complaining. Jean just could not understand it; Caren was so easy to get along with, yet she and Robert always seemed to be at each other's throats.

Jean took another cup of coffee with her into the living room. She used her address book to call Caren and Robert first. She might have to call Caren's cell phone and leave a message if she could not get her at home. Luck was with Jean, however, as Caren picked up the phone on the third ring.

After Jean identified herself Caren exclaimed ecstatically, "I am so glad to hear from you! It sure has been a while."

Jean asked, "How are things going at work?

Caren said "Oh, great! I work on the pediatric ward, and I think I want to adopt most of the kids. This is really where I belong."

When asked about Robert, Caren replied in a so-so voice, "His practice is booming, but I hardly ever see him. He even works two nights a week at the Emergency Care Center."

Jean thought to herself, "This is a marriage that makes me happy I am single," and then responded bluntly, "Why would he have to? I mean if his practice is booming, you two should be having no financial problems."

"Sadly," Caren responded, "it's the malpractice insurance we have to pay nowadays. It is nearly driving us out of the business. When will people figure out they cannot sue over every little scratch or bump or owee?"

Deciding to change the subject, Jean got to the point of her call. "Mary Carol and I thought it would be fun to get together for a potluck picnic on Sunday, just what's left of the gang here in Missoula. We thought we would have it in Mary Carol's backyard about 2:00. What do you think?"

As usual Caren responded enthusiastically, "What a great idea! The weather is supposed to be perfect, and I know I'd love to see everyone together again. I know I can come because I don't work weekends, but I am not sure about Robert's schedule. I know he doesn't have any patient in the hospital that needs special attention now, but as you know, that can change in a flash. I'll talk to him tonight about the picnic and give you a call back."

Jean assured, "That's fine. What do you think you could bring for the hungry horde?"

Caren laughed, "Oh, I have a great spiral ham, and what about some homemade rolls? Those could be Robert's donation...even though I made them."

"We would all be thrilled to have anything you wanted to bring since you're such an excellent cook, but those are great choices.

"To change the subject a bit, have you seen or talked to Max since he has been back in town?"

Caren answered, "I guess I have seen him once or twice in passing but haven't had the chance to talk with him. From what I could see, though, he looks fine."

Jean then asked, "Do you by any chance have Max's phone number?"

Caren said, "No, but I'll ask Robert this evening. He probably has it since he and Max are still such good friends."

Jean then got to the real point of her conversation, "Do you think Max and Beth will ever get back together again?"

Vehemently, Caren said, "I sure hope not! This break up is the best thing that ever happened to Max. That relationship emasculated him; the way Beth always insisted on taking care of every decision, big or small. He finally has a chance to gain some independence and self respect."

After hanging up the phone, Jean thought about what Caren had said. She really had defended Max strongly, almost out of character for Caren. Did she really mean the breakup would be good for Max, or did she mean it would be good for other reasons? Perhaps Jean had better watch the interaction between Caren and Max a little more carefully.

Next Jean had to call Crystal. She wasn't looking forward to it. She had always been a better friend to Bill than Crystal. There was just something about the woman that made Jean uneasy. Maybe it was her intensity. Well, she had better get to the task at hand.

When Crystal answered the phone and realized it was Jean, she was very friendly. "Oh, Jean, it has been ages since we have been able to get together, just the two of us. Would you be able to fit me in your busy schedule this weekend some time?"

Before Jean could even begin to say she would, Crystal gushed, "Oh, you won't believe the new, young artist, Connie Carlson, I have discovered in Kalispel. She has such incredible, undeveloped talent, which, of course, I plan to reveal to the world. She might even be another Russell or Remington. What an addition to the foundation!" With Bill's money and backing, Crystal had been able to start a foundation called Discovering New Western Artists. Through donations and grants, it was able to provide shows across the United States and even Europe for the newly discovered artists. "Are you sure you wouldn't like to donate a little something to the foundation?" Crystal implored in that wheedling voice Jean absolutely detested.

Jean gave her a rather firm, "No! I thought we had discussed this before. Remember I am living on retirement income now."

"Oh, that's right. I had forgotten," Crystal replied.

Trying not to be irritated, Jean got right to the point, "Mary Carol and I are planning a potluck picnic for the group here in Missoula on Sunday and were hoping you could join us about 2:00 in Mary Carol's backyard."

Crystal replied somewhat indifferently, "I really don't know. I don't have my planner with me. Could I call you back later today and let you know?"

"Of course," Jean replied, "and if you can come, could you please bring that pasta salad you are famous for? I cannot imagine a picnic without it!"

"I'd be happy to do that. Why don't I call you around 6:00 this evening," Crystal replied, her better mood seemingly restored.

Jean then asked what she felt was a critical question for all her phone contacts that began with a "C", "Have you seen or talked to Max lately?"

Crystal tartly replied, "I have not. Why do you want to know?"

Jean assured her, "I am worried about him since the breakup with Beth. I hope he is doing okay."

"Oh, I hear he is just fine, maybe too fine. But I have to go as I have an appointment with a potential buyer for one of my young protégés. I'll talk to you later. Bye." With that Crystal hung up.

Jean just sat there on the sofa with Mrs. Robinson curled in her lap and shook her head. What had Crystal meant by those snide remarks about Max? It was all very confusing. Maybe Jean had better watch more carefully the interaction between Max and Crystal. Something must have happened. They had always been close before. She also thought of Crystal's mention of the young artist Connie Carlson. She was definitely a "C" and lived in the same town as Max. Jean wondered if he knew her. Hmmmm.

Her last task for the morning was to call Max, a job she did not relish, especially since she was supposed to be there as "Beth's spy."

She was glad Mary Carol had had Max's number. Max answered on the first ring, almost as if he had been waiting for her call. Max said effusively, "How are you? I haven't seen you in so long. What have you been doing with yourself lately? I know you have been traveling quite a bit, but what else is new in your life?"

Jean laughed delightedly as she responded, "Well, I have been quite busy. As you know, three weeks ago I got back from a two week cruise in Europe from Vienna to Amsterdam. What an experience! I think it was absolutely the best vacation I have ever had. The cruise ship held only 150 people, so there were never crowds or long lines. There were daily tours you could elect to do, or you could simply stay on board and enjoy the water and perfect weather. I think my favorite tour was at the cathedral in Melk, Germany. It was incredible! I almost hated to get off in Amsterdam to fly home. It meant the end of an idyllic time.

"I also have started to write a book with two of my retired English teacher friends, Sally and Eileen. I don't know if we'll ever finish the thing, but we surely are having fun with the process."

Max listened intently and asked some probing questions. That was what Jean had always noticed about Max. He would listen to someone as if that person were the focus of his entire world. Perhaps that was the secret of his charm... That and the fact that he was an incredible hunk didn't hurt. If he and Beth did not get back together again, Jean bet it would not be long before some other female had him on her hook. Maybe it would be the infamous "C".

Back to business. Jean finally got around to the point of her call. "Max, Mary Carol and I are having a little get together on Sunday afternoon at 2:00 at Mary Carol's. We thought a potluck picnic in her back yard might be fun for the old gang here in Missoula. We certainly would like you to join us. What do you say?"

Max replied enthusiastically, "That sounds great. Do you want me to bring something? I have to warn you that since I am playing the role of bachelor, my culinary skills are just barely above boiling water and not burning it."

Laughing, Jean suggested, "Why not bring a couple cartons of pop and a nice bottle of wine. We'll be having ham."

Relieved Max said, "I know I can handle that.

"Say, since you are in town, why don't we get together tonight for dinner? I'd love to take you to Finn and Porter's at the Doubletree. They have great surf and turf there."

Jean was surprised and replied, "Why thank you, Max. I think that would be delightful. However, since I am Mary Carol's houseguest, shouldn't we invite her, too?"

There was quite a pause before Max responded, "Hmmm. I was hoping to spend some time alone with you, but, of course, you are right. Bring her along. How about I pick you up about 7:00?"

After she had hung up the phone, Jean wondered why Max had wanted to spend time alone with her. Did he want to talk about Beth or about a new girlfriend? Well, no matter what the reason, Jean knew it would be an interesting evening.

Chapter 6
Clues in the Coffee

Jean finished reading the Friday morning paper, the *Missoulian*, and smiled secretly to herself. The focus on national and regional news had improved through the years, and there were also more advertisements, but some things never change. The list of divorce decrees, marriage licenses, and court dates still provided profitable reading for the small town perusers of gossip. "Best not be calling the kettle black," she cheerily reminded herself. "But at least there was no listing for Max R. from Beth S. Milner. I wonder what is up with old Max?" Well, she certainly would find out something that night at dinner.

She wandered restlessly through the living room to the porch. "Hmm…10:30…Mary Carol won't be back from work for at least two hours. Surely she won't mind if I log on and pull up my AOL e-mail account. Beth is probably wondering what's going on, and even though I know precious little, it might make her feel better to know that I am thinking about her and trying to piece together the puzzle."

After booting up the computer, Jean signed on to AOL, used the guest account and her own password. "Now for the hard part," she thought. "What can I say that will be cheerful and realistic at the same time? Best just stick to the facts. Just the facts, Jean, just the facts."

Subject: Missoula Report
Date: 7/24/00 10:45AM Pacific Standard Time
From: MKSmiley2@aol.com
To: BMilner@my180.net

Dear Beth,
Arrived in Missoula yesterday afternoon and plan to visit with Max over dinner tonight.
Have also planned to round up the gang for a barbeque on Sunday. Maybe I can pick up some clues about who the mysterious "C" can be. Wish you could be with us, but maybe under the circumstances that would be a teeny bit awkward.
Have you come up with any other ideas? Or how about the computer? Any other information there? Know this must be a difficult time for you. Stay in touch and keep smiling.

Love, Jean

"Well, that certainly didn't eat up much time," Jean thought. "Maybe I'll take a quick walk toward campus and have a cup of coffee at that cute restaurant; what was it called? Oh, yes, the Back Door. Perhaps seeing young people in action will jump start my brain, and I'll come up with an inspiration about how to proceed."

Mrs. Robinson was lazing happily in the sunshine as Jean slipped quickly out the back door thinking about time and the havoc it could bring with no warning at all.

Crystal's life had certainly gone topsy-turvy when Bill unexpectedly drowned in May. She surely had not anticipated being a widow at age 60. Who would? On the other hand, independence had something to offer, too. The life of a single schoolteacher had taught Jean independence and had given her strength. Being alone is not really the end of the world for anyone.

Still it was just a short time ago it seemed they were all carefree kids with nothing more important to think about than what movie they would see on Saturday night or who had a date for the prom or what on earth they would wear to a Friday night dance. Now both Mary Carol and Crystal faced being alone. "Indeed, times change," Jean decided. "I wonder how Beth will be able to cope with living alone?"

As she strolled toward campus, Jean decided to concentrate on her mission in Missoula. Maybe with a little clever footwork, she could discover what was up with Beth and Max. No sense in turning yet two more lives upside down. After all, the golden years were surely on their way; all she needed to do was some fancy prospecting and maybe, just maybe, the Milners would see that over 30 years is a long time to throw away.

As she crossed the street and approached the coffee shop, Jean spied a couple happily gazing at each other as they sat on the deck. Hands entwined and eyes only for each other, their wholesome good looks somehow gave her new spring in her step. "Maybe young love and a tall hazelnut latte will inspire me with a plan of attack when we gather on Sunday afternoon."

"Jean, is that you? I didn't know you were in town, "exclaimed a robust male voice as she stepped inside the restaurant door.

"Well Bless Bess, I was looking forward to seeing you on Sunday, Robert, but this is an unexpected surprise. Do you have time for a quick cup of coffee?"

"I do have to stop and see my mother before I do my afternoon rounds at the hospital, but I can always spare a few minutes for an old friend. Goodness, when was the last time I saw you?" Robert inquired.

"I think it must have been when Bill died. It sure is hell to get old and have gatherings only for funerals. How did this ever happen to us? We should still be dragging the strip and going to outdoor movies. How is your mom, by the way?"

"We had to put her in extended care. Dad just couldn't offer the 24-7 care that she needs. What an insidious disease is Alzheimer's! It sneaks in on little cat feet, and pretty soon there is only the fog left. I try to see Mom at least twice a week; Caren makes an appearance when she can, but she finds the situation with Mom so depressing that it takes her weeks to get up enough nerve to go back."

"I didn't really see Bill before he died. How far had he progressed?"

Robert pondered a moment and replied, "It's terribly hard to assess someone unless you are with him constantly. According to Crystal he had good days and bad. Perhaps what took her by surprise the most was the rapid change from his happy, good-natured self to a grumpy, old man who took little pleasure in anything but fishing. Remember how much he loved music? That seemed to be the first to go. He often threw tantrums in the car when the radio was too loud, and he fought listening to tapes or CD's. He confessed to me that he was certain someone was following him. Sometimes paranoia becomes the worst enemy. He did make some good progress, however, with the new treatment. Unfortunately, it must not have been totally effective. I only wish I had been less optimistic and had tried to persuade him not to do that last damn fishing trip.

"Each person seems to react differently. Mother is pleasant enough, but she has no clue who I am or why Dad comes to visit her regularly. Surely some day medical research can find help. I do know there is a Swedish study of twins indicating that a regular regimen of an anti-inflammatory drug has been instrumental in preventing Alzheimer's. Maybe it does really boil down to 'Take two aspirin and call me in the morning.'"

Robert glanced at his watch and leaned over to give Jean a quick hug. "Sorry, old friend. I must run. Did you mention something about Sunday? I haven't talked to Caren about the weekend agenda, but that's nothing unusual. Sometimes I think we each have our own agenda and never the twain shall meet. Anyway, I'll see her tonight and see what's up. Hopefully, we can both see you and rake up some pleasant memories of yesteryear."

"Good to see you, Robert. Please tell Caren I'm looking forward to seeing both of you. I promise no gloomy stuff."

Jean drained the last of her latte and decided she had better forgo any further prowling about the campus. The bookstore could wait for

MURDER IS ONLY SKIN DEEP

another day. Mary Carol was probably already home and wondering where her houseguest had disappeared. The coffee had her revved up, but the conversation with Robert definitely was not a positive one. Neither had the topic of Max and Beth been broached, but there had scarcely been an opportunity. Probably Robert was out of the loop in that category as well. Men never did know what was happening right under their very noses. And what of the "separate agenda" comment? Surely a visit with Max would shed some light on the subject of his future with Beth, and maybe even reveal who "C" was, Jean hoped. "I only wish that my plan of attack involved something besides a new aspirin therapy."

Chapter 7
A Flash of Black

After a late and heavy lunch and a delicious bottle of wine, Jean and Mary Carol both decided to take a bit of a nap. Jean mumbled to herself as she trudged up the steps," I really don't think I should have had two glasses of wine. Oh, well, perhaps it will help me sleep deeply for my nap. Then I'll awaken refreshed and ready to go."

As the gentle tapping on the bedroom door drew Jean from her sound sleep, Mrs. Robinson started a most unladylike howl at the foot of the bed. Shushing her favorite feline, Jean moved sluggishly toward the door. "What does Mary Carol want?" she wondered. "I only lay down twenty minutes ago."

Opening the door, she frowned at Mary Carol. Mary Carol asked quickly, noting the expression on Jean's face, "I wondered when you were getting up. I hadn't heard any sounds up here."

Jean looked at her watch and exclaimed," Six fifteen! It can't be that late! Max will be here in about half an hour! My gosh! I slept over two hours. That's not like me!"

"I know," her sister-in-law responded calmly, "I figured you would need about half an hour to get ready, knowing how speedily you can dress, put your makeup on, and get your hair brushed."

"Oh, right," Jean said, finally wide-awake. She thought to herself,

"Amazing what a little squirt of adrenaline can do for a person." She then noticed the look on Mary Carol's face and the fact that she was not dressed for dinner either, unusual since she usually started getting ready an hour early. "What's up?" Jean questioned.

"I really don't think I am going to join you two tonight. I woke up with a terrible headache and feeling a little nauseous. It could be one of my migraines coming on. I took my medication, but it takes a while for it to kick in. I'll just stay home and rest if you don't mind," Mary Carol said quickly.

Jean exclaimed, "Oh, I am so sorry. Are you sure you want me to go? I'd be glad to stay home with you and make you some dinner... Whatever you want."

"No, you go ahead with Max. I just want peace and quiet for a few hours. Then I should be much better. You get ready, and I'll go downstairs to greet Max if he is early."

"Ok, if you are sure," replied Jean.

As she shut the door and turned to her "speedy" preparations, she wondered about Mary Carol. Usually there were signs that the migraine was coming on, but she had mentioned nothing about it. "Was she tense about something?" Jean wondered. "Well, there is no time to ponder the matter just now," she thought as she drew her favorite dress from the closet. She loved the silky feel of the aquamarine-colored dress and how it made her feel.

As she was just finishing her makeup and giving her hair a final fluff, Jean heard the doorbell downstairs. Then she heard Mary Carol greeting Max, so she started to slip on her dress shoes. "OOOO, my feet must be swelling in the heat," she thought disgustedly as she jammed the final foot in the exasperatingly small shoe. "What we women do for fashion and beauty," she sighed as she started down the stairs.

Max was standing in the foyer, chatting amiably with Mary Carol. He reached out and cupped her chin gently and said quite sadly, "I am really sorry you aren't feeling well and won't be joining us. You and I will have to make it another time," and then he winked at her. Jean was amazed as Mary Carol blushed deeply and looked away.

Jean sighed, "My God, I don't think the man knows the effect he has on women." Just looking at him reminded her of some of the statues she had seen two years ago in Rome, all incredible hunks of pulchritude. However, as she looked at Max, she thought of Beth and wondered, "Is his beauty just skin deep?"

Max looked up and spotted Jean. "Lord, woman, you look ravishing!" he exclaimed and moved quickly to hold both of her hands.

Jean just laughed and said, "Oh, you ole smoothie, you. Let's go into the living room for a second." As they all moved toward the living room, the doorbell rang again.

"I'll get it" responded Mary Carol as she rushed back to the door. Jean heard the door open and heard Mary Carol's surprised, "Crystal!"

As Mary Carol came back into the living room, Crystal followed her, smiling and looking absolutely gorgeous as usual. Jean briefly wondered if Crystal had someone fix her hair both morning and evening; she had never seen her shining, thick, black mane unkempt.

For some unknown reason, Crystal stopped dead in her tracks and stuttered, "Max, what are you doing here?"

Max stood up and put out both hands to warmly greet Crystal as he said, "Oh, I came by to take the girls out to dinner. However, Mary Carol does not feel well, so it's just Jean and me."

Crystal made no effort to reach out to Max as he greeted her, but rather turned to Mary Carol and inquired, "Are you all right?"

As Crystal was turned toward Mary Carol, Jean thought she saw a flash of black in the hallway. "Oh, no. It can't be Mrs. Robinson," Jean pleaded to herself. "I don't know why that usually sweet, serene pussycat hates Crystal as she does." As Jean moved toward Crystal to intervene, the flash of black was faster! Mrs. Robinson had her teeth implanted in Crystal's ankle before anyone could do anything to prevent it.

"O U C H!" Crystal yelped swinging her leg about wildly. Mrs. Robinson just seemed to be glued to her ankle. "Help me! Get this monster off me!!" Crystal screeched as she twirled about the room.

Finally Mrs. Robinson let go, gave a disgusted meow, and stalked from the room.

"Oh, my gosh! Are you okay?" Jean questioned.

"No, I am not okay," Crystal said sarcastically." How would you feel if that vicious animal attacked you every time you both are in the same room?"

Jean responded quite contritely," I am really sorry. She usually likes everyone. I don't really understand why she does that to you. Time got the better of me, and I never had the chance to put her back on the back porch. Here, let me get you some gauze, antiseptic, and bandages if you are bleeding."

"Of course, I am bleeding, you twit, but I will take care of myself, thank you." Crystal snarled at Jean. She then turned her back on Max and Jean as if they were not there." I just came over to tell MARY CAROL that I'll be here Sunday afternoon. Also, I have to go to Kalispell tomorrow to meet a new artist. I am trying to set up a tour for him since he is so gifted."

Max asked quietly," If he is from Kalispell, do I know him?"

"I doubt it. He really is quite a bit younger than you," Crystal said sharply. "I must be going. Oh, I forgot; Willy will be in town over the weekend. Do you think I could bring him to the picnic Sunday?"

"Of course, your son is welcome," Mary Carol replied. "The more, the merrier!"

With that Crystal swept out of the room, leaving everyone feeling somewhat stunned. Jean shook her head, gathered her purse, and said, "Well, Max. I guess we should be on our way." She turned to Mary Carol and asked, "Are you sure you are going to be okay?"

"I'll be fine. You two go on and have a wonderful evening. You have your key, don't you?" questioned Mary Carol. "I'll leave the porch light on if you're late."

"Yes, I do, thanks," replied Jean as she hugged Mary Carol goodbye.

Chapter 8
Max's Meandering Male Musings

Max guided Jean to his Chevy Blazer with a light touch on her elbow and opened the door on the passenger side for her with the easy grace of a gentleman accustomed to assisting a lady.

"He does have a way of making a lady feel special," Jean thought to herself and remembered how Beth had been bowled over more than thirty-five years ago by just that, along with Max's rugged good looks. She gave him a sideways glance as he crossed over to the other side of the van and swung himself easily into the driver's seat like the athlete he was. His tanned skin and dark hair contrasted dramatically with his blue eyes and white, even teeth as he smiled at her.

"I'm glad you're here, Jean, and I have to tell you I'm also happy to have some time alone with you." He said this in a rather somber tone and then added, "I'm hoping this means we can still be friends in spite of my leaving Beth after all these years."

Somewhat startled by Max's frankness, Jean answered, "Um, yes, Max, I think we can still be friends. I have to be honest with you, though, and admit that I was pretty shocked to hear from Beth that you were gone, not to mention puzzled about the whole thing." She chose her words carefully and felt a slight knotting in her stomach. Then wishing to change the subject, she added probably a bit too casually, "Nice rig you have here, Max. I always wondered if the dark tinting in the windows of some vehicles might impair one's vision, but I see it doesn't really do that at all."

"No," responded Max absently as he backed out of the driveway on to the street, "it simply offers a bit more privacy to the passengers inside, and, of course," he added rather hurriedly, "it cuts out the annoying glare of the sun and other bright lights that might cause a problem for the driver."

"Of course."

"I was able to get dinner reservations for us at Finn and Porter's as planned. I hope that meets with your approval," Max commented as he maneuvered through the traffic and headed toward the river.

"That sounds very nice, Max. If their food is as good as I remember it, I'm sure I can give the chef an A+."

"Always the teacher, aren't you, Jean? Tell me, are you enjoying your retirement, or do you feel a little lost when September rolls around? What have you been doing with all that time on your hands?" Max looked directly at her for a moment, smiled, and asked, "Now that you have more time for other things, what about men? Is there anyone special in your life?"

Jean thought to herself, "What is this? I'm the one who is here to find out about what this man has been up to, and here he is asking all the questions!" Slightly annoyed, she responded, "Well, Max, considering your situation, it seems to me that I ought to be asking you if you have some special person who prompted that."

Max's face flushed, and immediately Jean regretted her hasty words.

"Max, I'm sorry. That was rude of me and completely uncalled for. Please forgive me."

"No, Jean, after thirty-some years with Beth, who has been a friend of yours for longer than that, you probably are wondering what the hell is going on here. It's only natural. And I was out of line prying into your personal life. Let's just call a truce here. I won't ask you any personal questions, and you won't ask me any, and we'll just plan to stick to safe, and," he grinned at her, "more boring topics of conversation. Are we still friends?"

"Friends," Jean agreed, and thought, "Oh, great! Now I probably won't learn anything!"

After several minutes spent in discussing the weather, the changes that had taken place in Missoula since they were in high school, and other equally safe topics of conversation, they found themselves parking at the Doubletree Inn and making their way to the Finn and Porter Restaurant inside.

At the restaurant's entrance, Max told the young lady at the podium that he had made reservations for two.

"And the name, please?" the attractive blond asked, smiling up at Max with obvious admiration.

"Max Milner."

"Very good, Sir. Tracy, will you please show the Milners to their table?" the young blonde asked a pert, young waitress in the summer uniform of shorts and shirt.

Max said nothing to correct the impression that they were a married couple, Jean noted, but it really wasn't that important anyway, she thought.

"Certainly. Right this way, please." The young waitress smiled at Max and turned to lead the way to a table next to a window overlooking the river. Jean noticed that the other diners glanced up as they walked past them and smiled slightly, especially the ladies who happened to catch Max's eye.

When their waiter came to ask if they wanted to start with a drink, Jean ordered a glass of Chardonnay and thought to herself that it was just the ticket to help her relax and mellow out a bit. Max ordered a Scotch and water.

After Max ordered their dinners, it seemed to take a while for the staff to prepare them and bring them to their table, so they each had two more drinks before eating any food. Jean was, indeed, feeling quite relaxed, and Max was becoming more talkative.

He leaned over toward Jean and said rather confidentially, "I'm sure you really are wondering what happened between Beth and me to cause us to split up after all these years." Before Jean could respond, Max continued, "Things were not that great between us for a long time, Jean. We found that we really did not have that much in common. I liked to be active—ski, play tennis, work out—that sort of thing. Beth preferred staying home and tending to the fire, so to speak. She was a good cook and a devoted mother to the kids. But when it came to doing things with me, she would rather stay at home and cook or sew or read. I wanted to travel and see new places, but Beth was not interested in that either. Once the kids were grown and pretty much on their own, Beth and I hardly had anything to talk about. Oh, right here, please!" He flagged down a passing waiter. "Give me another Scotch and water, please. Jean, do you want another drink?"

"No thank you. I need food more than I need drink, I think."

At that moment their waiter came with their plates laden with delicious morsels—salmon, small new potatoes, and vegetables for Jean, and a juicy, pink-centered piece of prime rib with a baked potato and vegetables for Max. "Thank goodness!" thought Jean. "One more glass of wine without food, and I would start sliding to the floor." She secretly wondered how Max was doing as well as he was.

They ate in silence for a few minutes simply commenting occasionally on how delicious the food was.

After Max had finished another drink, he returned to the subject of Beth and their relationship. His speech was becoming slightly slurred. "You know, Jean," he said quietly and more intimately, leaning forward toward her and leaning his chin on his hand, "life's too short to deny one's self anything that would make him truly happy, don'tcha think? I mean, look at Crystal and Mary Carol, f'r instance. All of a sudden—boom! Both of their husbands—dead! Who would've thought? See what I mean about life's bein' short? So why stay in a relationship...a marriage...that isn't going anywhere? Beth deserves better. I'm not her type. And she was always tryin' to change me to suit her. That wasn't good either. It was time to end this charade. That's what it was...a charade.

Now we'll both be free to seek what each of us really wants before we find ourselves dead, too. Dead like Johnny and dead like Bill. Poor Johnny! Poor Bill!"

Jean was surprised when Max's eyes filled and spilled tears down his cheeks.

"Hey, Max," she said softly, "they're both in a better place now where there is no more sadness, no more tears. Come on, Max. Get hold of yourself. There was nothing anyone could do about the death of either one of them. It was completely out of our hands."

"Out of our hands where Johnny was concerned maybe, with that crazy guy crossin' over the center line and hittin' him head-on, but Bill's a different matter."

"Not really, Max. No one was there to stop Bill from slipping and having his waders fill with water, so he couldn't get up; only wearing a belt would have kept him afloat and stopped him from drowning; he must have chosen not to wear one. No one could have stopped Bill from drowning, Max. You know that. And maybe, just maybe it kept Bill from having to suffer a long time from the Alzheimer's, and Crystal, too, so maybe that turned out for the best for everyone concerned."

"Tha's egg-zackly right, Jean . It was for the best!" Max stated this with surprising emphasis in a louder tone of voice that caused two diners sitting nearby to turn and look at them.

"Shhh, Max. People are looking over here."

"Oops! Sorry, Jean . Still, even if it was for the best, poor Bill! Poor, helpless Bill!" And two more tears rolled down Max's cheeks.

"Max," Jean reached out and touched his hand. She spoke with compassionate firmness. "It's over. You must let go of this whole affair about Bill. You couldn't do a thing about what happened. None of us could."

"What do you mean...affair?" Max straightened up.

"Poor word choice, Max. This...this...thing that happened to Bill. The accidental drowning."

Max looked down at his plate and then looked at Jean and spoke earnestly, "Right, right, and I think you're right about it's maybe being better in the long run for Crystal, too. Poor, beautiful Crystal won't have to spend years taking care of poor Bill now. She can be free now, too."

Suddenly Max asked, "Have you heard anything from Beth lately? I figured that if anyone had, it would be you, Jean."

She wasn't expecting this question. How would she respond without lying?

"Well, yes, I've heard a little bit from her, Max. She sent me an e-mail telling me that there were some problems and that you had left, but that's about all." Jean added to herself, "I did say 'that's about all.' I didn't say 'it was all!'"

"Do you know how she's doing?"

"I think she's upset, but that's understandable."

Max sighed, "Yes, it is." He flagged down another waiter and asked for another Scotch and water.

"Max, don't you think you've had enough? Maybe a little bit too much? Jean asked softly.

"No, I don't. But I am going to ask you to drive me home, and I'll call a cab to take you back to Mary Carol's."

After Max finished his Scotch and water,he asked for the bill, paid it with a generous tip, stood up unsteadily, and pulled out Jean's chair for her. He took her hand, tucked it in his arm, and smiled somewhat ruefully at her. "Thanks for helping t' keep me steady."

They walked slowly out of the restaurant to the parking lot. Max opened the door to side, got in, and promptly fell asleep.

When they arrived at Max's apartment, Jean breathed a silent prayer of thanks that it was on the ground floor, and with Max leaning heavily on her, she took his keys, opened the door, and guided him to the living room couch. There she positioned Max on the couch with a pillow under his head and took off his shoes. She found a blanket on the foot of his bed in the bedroom,covered him, and called a cab for herself. So much for Max's calling one for her!

On the way back to Mary Carol's, Jean reviewed the events and conversations of the evening, thinking there were a lot of things for her to sort through, but she would save that for morning.

After paying the cab driver, Jean let herself into the house and soon discovered that Mary Carol was not there. One more thing to wonder about!

"What next?" she asked herself as sank down on the couch wearily with her head in her hands.

At that moment she heard the back door open, and Mary Carol appeared, slightly breathless and with a flushed face and bright eyes. She was wearing a peach-colored jogging outfit and her walking shoes.

Jean looked at her carefully. "You seem to have made a remarkable recovery," she said rather ruefully. "Too bad you didn't get over your headache in time to go to dinner with Max and me. You missed a pretty interesting evening."

Mary Carol sat down next to Jean quickly. "Oh, Jean, I really am sorry. I did have a headache coming on, so I took some of my medication and lay down for a while and started to feel better. Then when Fred called and asked if I wanted to walk tonight, I said yes, so we went out for a short walk. I know I should have told you about Fred in the first place. I really don't know why I have felt so hesitant about doing that except that at first it didn't seem quite right to be spending time with another man, but now I'm beginning to realize that Johnny wouldn't want me to be alone, and he would want me to be happy, too."

"I'm sure he would, Mary Carol," Jean said with conviction. "Now who's this Fred you're talking about?"

"Fred Williamson, the Montana State Patrolman who came to tell Crystal about Bill's death. Fred and I became acquaintances after that, and then friends. We have been seeing each other pretty regularly, and we like to walk and jog together. Oh, and while we were walking tonight, I invited him to the picnic Sunday. I hope that's okay with you." She looked at Jean questioningly.

"Oh, Mary Carol, I'm so relieved that you are home and all right, and I'm glad you're happier, too!" She gave her sister-in-law a hug and then sighed, "I'm exhausted. Let's go to bed, and you can fill me in on all the details tomorrow while we get ready for the picnic." She cleared her throat and added, "At least all the details you care to tell me!" and then gave Mary Carol a broad wink.

Chapter 9
I Never Would Have Dreamed

The girls had just enjoyed a leisurely breakfast on the back porch and were still lingering over coffee and the newspaper. Somewhat lazily and reluctantly, they realized that they needed to made plans for the day's activities; Mary Carol yawned mightily and started the ball rolling. "O.K., my friend, this picnic is going to require a bit of effort here; best we get crackin'. Let's start with a grocery list, and maybe we can get the shopping done before lunch. That will give us this afternoon to bake up a few goodies. Thank goodness my stupid headache is gone. Just wish I felt a little more industrious."

Jean looked at her friend with some concern. "I am so sorry you had to suffer through another migraine. Do you ever have a clue about what causes them to drop in so unceremoniously?"

Mary Carol replied somewhat nonchalantly, "You know, I've put up with these puppies for so many years that I guess I just accept them. Sometimes I think it's too much rich food and sometimes it's stress. It's just hard to put my finger on the cause each time. Guess I'm getting a little old to hope that I'll outgrow them."

The notion of stress took Jean a bit by surprise. Surely her visit and the prospect of entertaining had not set her friend into a decline, had it? Well, she would try to do as much as possible in the preparation department and hopefully Mary Carol would be feeling a bit spryer tomorrow. "Ok, ok, a list is in order. Suppose we find peaches and apples, and I'll whip up a couple of pies? If we have pies and ice cream for dessert, we should have plenty to eat."

"I think we do need some munchies before the real eating begins," Mary Carol suggested. "How about if we fix a fruit plate and a veggie tray and have some chips and dip? I found a wonderful new mix that just requires stirring it up with some sour cream."

"Sounds good to me," Jean responded. "Speaking of sour, I do hope that Crystal is a bit more congenial tomorrow. She was down right nasty last night. Do you think seeing Max unexpectedly set her into a tizzy?"

"Oh, I don't think so. Maybe she's just feeling overwhelmed with her son coming in and a trip to Kalispel in the making. Perhaps it could also be related to seeing Max and you and me. You know, the old gang and no Bill. I remember that blank feeling myself after Johnny died. It's as if you are sure he'll be coming in the door at any minute and will be so glad to see everyone."

"Maybe so. Grief certainly affects everyone differently. Sounds as if she is keeping plenty busy, but maybe busy doesn't always cut it. I hope it will be good for her to have her son around this weekend." Then Jean asked, "Have Crystal's kids been very attentive?"

"I know they call frequently, and Willy has been here a couple of times since Bill died. He helped her clear out his dad's things and settle some of the estate matters. I understand that was no easy chore because Bill was quite confused at times, and Crystal never did really have a head for numbers or figures. You and I both know she enjoys spending money much more than accounting accurately for it."

"Let's do the best we can to cheer her up. Maybe new memories will soften the grief a bit. I also think I'd better be VERY sure that Mrs. Robinson is well confined. I could even put her in her travel cage in my room. That should surely be safe enough. Well," Jean stood up, "the produce aisle is beckoning. Shall we complete a hasty toilette and be off before the day heats up and makes the kitchen unbearable?"

Later as Mary Carol and Jean perused the peaches and discussed the merits of a fresh peach pie or a baked one, they were greeted heartily by an old schoolmate, Nancy Armison. She had been a class behind them, and after her marriage had remained in Missoula and occasionally bumped into Mary Carol for a chat about "remember when" or "have you heard about...." Nancy had aged beautifully. Her blonde, curly hair and trim figure certainly did not belie her age.

"Jean, how good to see you!" Nancy said enthusiastically. "Are you just in town for a visit?"

"Yes, just for the weekend," Jean replied. "I needed a reprieve from my garden, and Mary Carol and I do enjoy staying in touch. I've also touched bases with Max Milner and Crystal Pemberton."

"Max? I didn't realize he was in Missoula. Have he and Beth moved from Kalispell?" Nancy inquired.

"Well, actually, Max is here on his own. Beth is still in Kalispell, at least for now," Mary Carol offered.

Nancy looked as if she might wish to pursue this topic but then galloped on to something that she evidently felt was more salacious. "And how is Crystal doing? Do you know if they ever figured out exactly what happened to Bill? How long as it been now? May, wasn't it?"

Scarcely stopping for a response Nancy plunged on, "A detective friend of mine told me on the Q.T. that they were wrapping up the investigation. Apparently the lengthy time in the water made the autopsy somewhat inconclusive. Nevertheless, there didn't really seem to be any evidence of foul play, and there seemed to be no indication of a homicide."

Mary Carol and Jean exchanged horrified looks. Jean dropped the peach she had been selecting and gulped hurriedly. "Well, you do know that Bill was suffering from Alzheimer's and had periods of true confusion. Apparently the fishing trips proved to be one of those times with a rather disastrous result."

Nancy nodded sympathetically. "And how about Crystal? How is she doing? I've heard that she manages to stay very busy with her art dealings and young artist friends." Nancy seemed to smirk a bit as she said this.

YVONNE DEITZ, VIKKI MOORMANN, SUSAN SCHREIBER

"Yes," Mary Carol replied, "fortunately Crystal does have her art interests to keep her busy. It's so good to see you Nancy, but we have a million things to accomplish this morning, and it's almost noon, so if you'll excuse us, we'd better get going."

"Have a good visit, Jean. Stop by if you have time. You know I live a block from where I grew up, on the east side of the campus."

Reeling somewhat from the gossipy exchange, the ladies finished up their shopping and made their way home. Neither seemed anxious to discuss the possibilities that Nancy's news had introduced. Instead they threw themselves into the throes of pie baking; peeling, mixing, and rolling seemed preferable to contemplating the notion of the untoward death of an old friend.

Finally when the spicy, cinnamon aroma of freshly baked pies filled the air, Mary Carol tugged off her apron and summoned Jean to the back porch. "Come on, My Friend. We have finished for the day. We are going to have a glass of wine. I'll make a salad in a bit, and we'll have a light supper and an early night."

"Your wish is my command," Jean agreed. "You open the wine, and I'll bring the glasses."

"A cool evening breeze wafted through the screen, and the two friends contentedly assessed their day. "A pretty good effort for two old girls," Mary Carol began. "All we really have to do tomorrow is get the table ready and put some ice in my copper tub. So, what did you think of Nancy's bombshell?"

Jean blinked at the sudden change of topic—from pies and tubs to notions of foul play, but she knew the topic had been brewing in the back of each of their minds all afternoon. "Well, you know Nancy has always been a bit of a gossip. Even in high school I remember one had to be careful of bestowing any kind of confidence. I can't imagine that Crystal wouldn't have mentioned any kind of suspicion to you. You were pretty involved with the whole sordid affair about Bill' weren't you?"

"Not really, Jean. Of course, I was there at the beginning when we got the news, and we all helped with the funeral. But after that, I don't know. Crystal just seemed to withdraw and was dashing off hither and thither with her art business. Our schedules never seemed to mesh really, and, to tell the truth, I don't see a lot of her."

After another glass of wine and some cheese and crackers, the ladies decided to bag the salad and call it a day. "I have a great book I really would like to finish," Jean offered. "And I know a good night's sleep will benefit us both. Let's hit the sack."

Even Mrs. Robinson seemed to be in agreement. She bounded up the steps to Jean's room and as quickly as you could say Jack Robinson, the purring cat was nestled in beside her mistress. Jean read for a bit and finally turned out the light to drift off into an uneasy sleep. She tossed and turned awakening with a start with a clear vision of the dream that wakened her—a raging stream, a snaggly log, and suddenly she was under the water grasping frantically for the surface. Just as she reached hopelessly for the top, she woke in a cold sweat. Not even the sound of Mrs. Robinson's soft breathing could comfort her as she tried forlornly to sleep once more.

Chapter 10
To "C" or Not to "C"

Gathering the rest of the utensils and plates needed for the picnic, Jean shook her head in frustration and thought," Boy! Some detective I am. I have been here since Thursday, and it's already Sunday afternoon. I don't even have a clue who the infamous "C" of e-mail fame is yet. Beth is going to be mighty disappointed in me."

Jean left the kitchen area through the open door and entered the back porch but paused for a moment and through the screen door perused the group laughing and talking in Mary Carol's back yard. She thought to herself, "Maybe I was totally wrong, and 'C' isn't among this group Maybe it's someone I haven't even met or heard of yet." She glanced over to where Max was standing, slightly set apart from everyone else yet still a part of the whole. He had another bottle of his favorite beer, some sort of dark, brown stout, in his hand and a rather melancholy look on his face. Jean mused, "I really think he is drinking too much. After that bizarre dinner we had Friday night, I am almost embarrassed to talk to him." Suddenly Max turned and looked straight at her. Flushing a bit, she opened the screen door and went out into the yard.

As she proceeded toward the table, she passed Willy, Crystal and Bill's son, who was spending the weekend next door with his mother.

"The poor guy," Jean thought, "He certainly was severely sunburned yesterday!" She reflected on what he had told her when he first came over this afternoon.

"I just cannot believe I did this to myself," Willy had lamented. "I had originally intended to just rest in the sun for about a half an hour. I went out to the pool, put on some sunscreen that I found upstairs in Mom's drawer, and settled into the lounge chair. I thought I would just close my eyes for a few seconds and enjoy the warmth. The next thing I knew it was five hours later, and I guess you could say I was par-broiled. I never have had anything like that happen to me before! By 10:00 o'clock last night I was so sore I could not sleep or move or anything. Mom wasn't back yet, so I called Margie at home in Spokane to figure out what to do. All the years we have been married, she always has known what to do when I am injured. She remembered when she was younger, her mom had covered a bad sunburn with tea-soaked towels, and that had really helped. So I just filled the bathtub with tepid tea water and settled in. I actually think I slept a bit. To say Mom was surprised when she came home late last night and found a whale looking like a boiled lobster is an understatement! She lathered me in aloe lotion and put me to bed. When I got up this morning and Mom saw me, she suggested I keep the affected areas moist with some lotion she had. That has helped somewhat, but I really think I will have a rough week!"

Jean had sympathized with him. She thought, "Poor Willy! No matter what he does, it just never seems to turn out right. He is the total antithesis of his parents." Both his parents had been ambitious, successful, and strikingly good-looking. Bill had been tall, lean, and had chiseled features. Of course, Crystal is still a beautiful woman with that gorgeous, thick black hair and willowy figure. Willy, on the other hand, was a rather nondescript, short, pudgy guy one might not remember meeting ten minutes later.

As Willy turned to look up at her, Jean gave him a warm smile. Though she didn't think it would be possible, Willy seemed to blush and turn an even darker red.

Placing the utensils and plates on the table, Jean looked across the yard to where Robert and Caren were standing. Once again they

59

seemed to be having some sort of disagreement. Jean went around to the other side of the table so she could hear but not seem to be listening.

"I do not especially care what you think!" Caren growled at Robert. "I don't know who told you such a thing. Believe me, if I were going to see another man while I was married to you, you would be the FIRST person I'd tell!"

"Oh, come on," Robert sneered. "You can't tell me it has never crossed your mind...to seek greener pastures while I am working my butt off trying to provide for our future."

"Yeah," replied Caren snidely, "We'll have a great future together after we have spent nearly thirty years always apart because YOU ALWAYS HAVE TO WORK!"

The next thing Jean realized was that Caren had rushed past her, nearly knocking her over. Caren had gone directly to Max who asked, "What now, Baby?" He then had put his arm around her and walked her toward the roses, talking softly to her.

"Hmmm," Jean thought, "Maybe I do know who the mysterious 'C' is."

Everyone had stopped talking at Caren's rather abrupt and strident statement to Robert. Even though Caren and Robert had fought like cats and dogs all their married life, they always seemed to be over the disagreement pretty quickly. Embarrassed to be caught listening, everyone started to jabber at once.

Jean walked toward the beautiful, new waterfall and rock garden Mary Carol had put in her backyard that summer. She and Crystal were talking quietly as Jean approached.

"My, that certainly was embarrassing," Mary Carol said sadly. "I wonder if they ever do go a day without arguing about something."

"I don't think so," said Crystal. "They seem to always be looking for something to disagree about."

"I just don't get it. I would want warmth, serenity, and fun in my marriage," Jean responded as she looked first at Max and Caren and then at Robert who was still glowering.

Crystal said snippily, "Well, that certainly explains why you never married," and walked across the yard to sit with Willy.

Jean lowered her voice and confided to Mary Carol," God knows I have tried, but I find it very difficult to like that woman."

Mary Carol laughed and said, "Oh, you get used to her. She's not that bad. It's all a facade."

Both Jean and Mary Carol turned as they heard the creaking of the side gate, indicating another guest had arrived. Jean caught just a brief glance of Mary Carol's face as Mary Carol rushed toward the gate. Mary Carol looked so happy! Jean was happy to see it was Fred Williamson and even more pleased to see him reach out for Mary Carol's hand, pull her close, and give her a warm kiss.

Mary Carol's warm, lilting voice called out, "Everyone, I want you to come and meet Fred Williamson. You might remember him, as he was two years behind us in school."

As everyone moved to greet Fred, Jean smiled to herself as she noticed Fred never let go of Mary Carol's hand. "So this is why she seems so much happier. I am so glad for her." Jean noticed Mary Carol looked hesitatingly towards her; Jean smiled warmly and moved toward the couple with the others.

After everyone had had a chance to greet Fred, they decided to eat. Jean later thought, "The food, as usual, was absolutely delicious and enough to feed at least an army. Finally after dessert, people started to settle down into small groups for some laid back conversation while their food digesed. I think I'll just make my rounds and see if I can pick up any useful information."

She took the chair next to Willy. He had been talking quite seriously with Max. Willy turned to Jean and said, "I was just thanking Max for all the help he has given Mom since Dad passed away. He is always there for her, and I just want him to know how much we both appreciate it!"

Jean thought Max looked rather chagrined as he said, "Oh, Willy, it really is nothing. It is what any good friend would do. Excuse me, I need another beer," and he got up and walked toward the ice chest.

Willy looked a moment at Max as he walked away, turned to Jean and said, " No matter what he says, I really think he saved my mom's life." They were quiet for a while, and then Willy said, "Excuse me. It's time for another dose of lotion, or I'll be twitching violently in a half hour." He rose stiffly from his chair, gathered up a large bottle of clear lotion from beneath his chair, and headed toward the house.

Jean left her chair and moved toward another group, this time Mary Carol, Fred, Caren, and Robert. Apparently Caren and Robert had made up. As she approached the group, she thought she heard Robert quietly ask Fred," Are you really sure there was nothing to indicate foul play?" When Robert realized Jean might have heard him, he said in a louder voice, "Are you sure there was no foul ball in the third inning?' As Jean sat down, Robert told her," We were just talking about the last Seattle Mariner's game. I still think there was something going on in the outfield that the umps missed."

Jean didn't think that was what Robert had said but just smiled and nodded. The conversation stayed on the baseball topic, so she finally moved to another group. Willy was back from the lotion anointing, and he and Crystal were talking.

Willy said, "I'm sorry, but I am going to have to leave for Spokane in about an hour. Are you sure you are going to be okay, Mom?"

"Of course I'll be okay. I have been doing pretty well so far. Don't worry about me, Honey," Crystal replied. "I think I had better help Mary Carol pick things up here, and then we can go home so you can pack."

Jean suggested, "Don't get up, Crystal. I'll do it."

Crystal once again ignored Jean and started to gather some of the dishes. Jean just sighed and started to gather some of the trash, bottles, and cans. Once she and Crystal started doing that, others realized that it was time to leave and wished Jean a safe trip home. Most had departed by the time Jean gathered the last of the litter and headed for the kitchen. She had just entered the back porch when she looked through the kitchen window and saw Max and Crystal kissing. Jean was so surprised, she stopped in her tracks.

Crystal broke away from Max and said, "No, Max. Someone will see!" She rushed into the hallway leading to the front door.

Jean did not want to be discovered spying on Max and Crystal, so she quietly tiptoed back outside. She stood there for a moment just thinking, "I'll be darned. Maybe the mysterious "C" is Caren or Crystal. I wonder which one?

Chapter 11
Foul or Fair?

After a leisurely breakfast the next morning, the two sisters-in-law lingered over a second cup of coffee and talked about the picnic and the people who were there that they had known for such a long time who were there.

"Thanks so much for letting me come over for the past few days and see how everyone is doing, Mary Carol. Except for a few uncomfortable moments with Max at dinner the other night, I really enjoyed myself, and even that was interesting, to say the least. And by the way, it warms my heart to see you and Fred together and see you looking so happy once again. It really is good to know that life does go on even after a loss and to know that life can be good again, too."

"Oh, Jean, I'm so glad you came. It has been so good to be together again." Mary Carol gave a little sigh and continued, "I can't tell you how relieved I am that you approve of my relationship with Fred. You and I have been such good friends long before Johnny and I were married, and I really am glad that this new turn my life is taking hasn't seemed to do anything to jeopardize our friendship. I want us to be sisters always, no matter what." Mary Carol's eye glistened as a small tear rolled out of the corner of one of her eyes and landed on the front of her robe.

"You know how much I loved Johnny. I didn't think it would be possible to have so much feeling for another man again after Johnny died. At first, I felt a little guilty about the feelings I was having for Fred. When he started calling me on the phone, I would try to put down the excitement I felt at just hearing his voice and tell myself I had no business feeling that way. Then I realized I really wasn't married anymore with Johnny gone, and after that I began to be more comfortable and decided to just wait and see what would happen next with Fred and me." She smiled at Jean and added, "He is a very dear friend, and he makes me feel very happy."

"It shows, and I think it's wonderful!"

Jean glanced at her watch, gave a little sigh, and said, "Well, good as it's been, I think Mrs. Robinson and I had better be hitting the trail for home again. The chores I left behind will be waiting for me, and I don't want to take advantage of my neighbor' kindness and make a pest of myself." She stood up and began clearing the table of the breakfast dishes.

An hour and a half later the two women were saying their goodbyes, and Mrs. Robinson was comfortably grooming herself on her blanket in the front seat of Jean's car.

"Give me a call when you get home, okay?" asked Mary Carol.

"Will do. You take good care of yourself, and we'll be in touch. We need to plan our next get-together before the snow flies, don't you think?"

"Absolutely! Have a safe trip, and we'll talk soon."

Jean backed carefully out of Mary Carol's driveway, gave a final smile and a wave, and she and Mrs. Robinson were on their way home.

As the miles passed by, Jean's thoughts drifted from warm and happy thoughts about her sister-in-law and her new love to the nagging purpose of her visit to Missoula in the first place—news about Max and the infamous "C."

"What am I going to tell Beth?" she said out loud, to which Mrs. Robinson answered with a firm "Meow!"

"Oh, sure, easy for you to say, Mrs. R. What do you think? Should we invite Beth to come to Spokane Valley and plan a few pleasant things to do, so she can focus on something besides this unpleasant business with Max and their former "charade", as he called it?"

Mrs. Robinson calmly groomed her right front paw and responded with another "Meow," uttered in a rather matter-of fact tone.

"I swear, Mrs. Robinson, sometimes I think you are almost human and really do understand everything I say."

The plump, shiny, black cat looked up at Jean, meowed again, and then curled up with her head on her front paws and closed her eyes.

"All right, Mrs. R., that's what we will do. As soon as I get caught up from this trip, we'll ask Beth to come over for a visit. In the meantime, let's think about "C" and who that might be."

Since the marriage had not been good for a long time, according to Max, and since Beth felt that his affair with "C" had been going on for some time, Caren or Crystal seemed like logical suspects.

Caren and Robert were not exactly your picture of the perfect loving couple the way they argued so readily, and Caren had rushed straight to Max at the picnic after she and Robert had their little tiff. "I wonder what prompted that little outburst in the first place," wondered Jean. Max had been quite solicitous when Caren approached him, had referred to Caren as "Baby", and seemed most eager to offer her comfort. "And yet," Jean thought out loud, "Caren and Robert acted as if nothing out of sorts had ever occurred a little while later. And," she sighed, "that has seemed to be their usual style ever since they have been together."

Then there was the kiss between Crystal and Max. "Now that looked pretty fishy to me!" Jean spoke those words loudly enough that it awakened Mrs. Robinson, who responded with a rather annoyed sounding "Meow!"

"So you think so, too, hmmm, Mrs. R.?"

Jean's thoughts then went to Crystal and Bill, wondering what their marriage had been like. They had made a striking couple, and Bill had always seemed proud to be seen with his beautiful wife, but their interests were not always in tune with each other. Bill had loved his fishing trips and treks into the woods. He was a real nature lover, whereas Crystal's first love seemed to be not so much real nature, but the reproductions of nature and other objects in paintings and sculpture. Closely connected to that was her love of collecting fine art objects and beautiful, expensive pieces of jewelry, which Bill had readily given to her. Was Crystal deeply in love with Bill, or did she love what Bill was able to give her?

Jean's thoughts then went to Willy at the picnic and what he had told her about how he really felt that Max had saved Crystal's life after Bill died. Max had, indeed, been there for Crystal, spending time with her, helping with the details of transferring finances into her name, and dealing with numerous other business arrangements that needed to be dealt with. "I don't want to make any accusations without proof, though," Jean reasoned. "We are simply going to have to be patient about this 'C' person, whoever she is, be alert, and keep our eyes and ears open. In the meantime, I think the first priority is to help Beth get her life in order and try to help her simply to feel better."

As she drove along the highway, Jean was drinking in the view of the forest-covered mountains, which were becoming more abundant as she traveled west, and being amazed, as she always was, at the number of times she drove on bridges crossing over the winding Clark Fork River.

As she got nearer to the Montana/ Idaho border, Jean decided to stop for lunch and stretch her legs at the picturesque $10,000,000 Silver Dollar Bar. Since Mrs. Robinson had made use of her portable litter box on the floor of the back seat, Jean opened the door to the cat carrier on the back seat and urged the cat through the door and to the soft pillow in the "cage" so she would be out of sight of curious passers-by. Mrs. Robinson protested slightly at this, but soon curled up comfortably in the carrier and yawned.

Since it was a weekday, the crowd of people in the gift shop section of the restaurant/bar was not as large as it usually was, and Jean was able to make her way quickly through the shop to a booth in the restaurant. After ordering a sandwich and soft drink, she looked about and watched the people, something she always found interesting.

Two couples who appeared to be in their mid-forties seated themselves in a booth directly behind Jean, and she was able to hear their conversation. They were discussing an item that had appeared in a local newspaper and apparently involved someone both couples knew.

"Terrible, isn't it?" one of the women lamented. "I don't understand how anyone could bring himself to actually take the life of another human being, let alone someone to whom you were married!"

"Happens all the time," one of the men said matter-of-factly. "Common occurrence in the bigger cities if you were to read their newspapers."

"Still," the other woman protested, "It's an awful thing to do, and a pretty extreme way to get yourself out of a marriage. There's always divorce, which is a heck of a lot more humane, it seems to me!"

"Some people just get desperate, and they can't see past their own noses, and then when there's another person they are involved with and want to be with, they'll do whatever it takes to get what they want," the second man reasoned. "Add the influence of drugs to all that, and they really don't care what they do. In fact, they are beyond reason. It's pretty tragic all the way around and all too common these days, I'm afraid."

Jean agreed wholeheartedly with the man's remarks and felt grateful that she didn't know of anyone who would take such drastic actions, at least, she hoped not.

After Jean finished eating, paid her bill, and made a trip to the ladies' room, she walked around the building a couple of times to get a little exercise and stretch, and then she headed back to her car, where Mrs. Robinson was dozing in the cat carrier. She decided to just let her sleeping cat lie for the rest of the trip home, and she headed to the freeway entrance.

The conversation of the couples in the restaurant stuck in Jean's mind along with the news she had heard this weekend about an investigation connected to Bill's death and set her mind to working again. She also remembered Robert's words about "foul play", which made her feel very uncomfortable. What if Bill's death was not an accident? What if someone wanted Bill out of the way? What if that someone were Crystal? "Oh, boy, Jean, you are really letting your imagination work aren't you?" she chided herself. "Mom and Dad always told you when you were a kid that you had a really great imagination, and that was a good thing when it came to being creative as an English teacher. However, when it comes to real life it can sometimes be a disadvantage, especially the way you sometimes have a tendency to make mountains out of molehills! Better be careful with this."

Jean reached on the dashboard for the radio button and tried to find a music station she liked that didn't have too much static on the highway. She managed to find one that wasn't too bad that was playing some old songs that she liked. She heard some she could sing along with, and that was kind of fun, she thought. "Dreamin'" came on, and she sang along for a while and then was reminded of the nightmare she had, which made her feel somber again.

Max's infidelity, the identity of "C," and Bill's death—foul play, or was it simply an accident? What did it all mean?

Chapter 12
The Green, Green Grass of Home

Jean approached the Argonne Exit with a touch of barn fever; she had spent the last three hours hashing and rehashing possibilities, analyzing personalities, and remembering the past. The comfort of her own home and routine would be a pleasant "diversion," she thought ironically. "How soon we forget," she mused; it was just a few short days ago that she enthusiastically escaped from weeding and watering to come to the aid of her old friend, Beth. "Do wish I could have some definitive news for her," Jean thought sadly. "Somehow, I feel more befuddled than anything else."

Mrs. Robinson, however, didn't feel confused. She seemed to sense that home was close, and she stretched and yowled a bit from the confines of the cat carrier. "Yes, indeed, my feline friend. Home is just around the corner, and soon you'll be prowling happily about in familiar territory. You are a great traveler, but enough is enough. Right?"

As she rounded the corner and approached the driveway, Jean was glad to see that the grass was still green, the flowers still in bloom, and even the petunias in the window boxes seemed perky and welcoming. "Yup. It's always true: Be it ever so humble, there's no place..." Her philosophizing was interrupted as she saw her neighbor, John Houck come through the gate on the side yard. "He must have been changing the sprinkler in the back," Jean decided and pulled into the driveway with a sigh of relief.

"Howdy, neighbor," Jean greeted him happily. "I see that you have been hard at work. The yard and planters look great. Thanks so much for taking care of them for me."

Well, howdy, yourself, Jeannie. You know I was glad to do it. We have had a spurt of fairly warm weather, and I would hate to see your yard dry up. It's good to have you home. Successful trip?"

"In some ways, yes, it was very successful. In yet another way, however, it opened a giant can of worms," Jean responded forlornly. Somehow she could not put away the mental quandaries that had been with her for the last 200 miles.

"Tell you what," John grinned at her, "even with those worms you have, it's a little late in the day for fishing. Why don't you let me help you take your luggage inside, and while you freshen up, I'll go next door and fix us a long, cool drink. I'd even be game for a bite of dinner at Tony Roma"s. What do you say?"

The comfort of someone else making a decision and taking charge was almost overwhelming; the threat of tiredness seemed to evaporate. "I just need to get Mrs. Robinson settled and splash some cool water on my face. I think you might be just what the doctor ordered," Jean answered happily. "I can be ready in 20 minutes."

After they finished a tall gin and tonic on John's back deck, they made their way toward Tony Romas, a popular dinner spot only a few miles from their Spokane Valley homes. Settling comfortably into a booth, Jean realized she was hungry. "I wonder if mental energy burns calories," she pondered. "Salad and barbequed ribs will fit the bill for me," she decided.

"Now what about those worms, Jean? You know I am a good listener and sometimes a second fisherman can still the waters and make some sense of things."

Jean couldn't help chuckling at the aptness of his allusion and wondered almost helplessly where to begin. She did trust John implicitly and suddenly realized that his police background might be just the ticket for helping to answer the myriad of questions that continued to while away in her addled brain.

After Jean had briefed him quickly about Beth's e-mail and the reason for her trip to Missoula, she launched into some detail about the result of her findings there. She introduced him quickly to her Montana friends, gave him some background about the past and present connections for the cast of characters, and related the conversation that she and Mary Carol had had with Nancy Armison in the grocery store. She continued with some detail about the events that had taken place at the picnic. Somehow, however, she stopped just short of a rehash of her haunting dream.

"So you see, John, I went to Missoula to sleuth about and find the identity of the mysterious 'C.' I came home with two possibilities for the answer to that question, but more importantly with other questions that seemingly have no ready answers. I guess if I cut to the chase, what I really need to verbalize has to do with death, murder, homicide——not a very pleasant kettle of fish."

"Well, young lady, I learned through many years of experience that most questions do have answers. Not always the ones we want to hear. Not always the ones that make us happy. Not always the ones that we could even imagine. So I propose that we set about on a course of finding those answers and then determine what to do about them."

Jean couldn't help smiling. The very maleness of John's reasoned response was indeed a contrast to the whirling emotions that had plagued her all day long. Perhaps his masculine reasonability, his police experience, and maybe most of all his objectivity and ability to stand back and plot out a course of action would help her put things into perspective and at least begin to know what kind of explanation she was going to offer Beth. After all, that was really how this had all started out and what she had promised to investigate.

"OK, Mr. Homicide Man. Where do we begin?"

"With the facts, Jeannie, with the facts. Now this fella, Bill, was reported missing and ultimately found in the river where he had been fishing. There is on file a death certificate, possibly a coroner's investigation, and an autopsy report. An autopsy would certainly have been done if the family had requested it, or if there were any suspicion of homicide. These records are available if the case is not under current investigation. It sounds to me as if the matter has been laid to rest. Your policeman friend, Fred, indicated that there was no evidence of foul play, and I would suspect that the ruling was that it was an accidental drowning."

"So you're suggesting that we check out these reports to see if there was anything that was overlooked?" Jean queried

"I'm not so sure that overlooked is the right word, Jean. But coupled with the information that you have picked up, there might be some new interpretations that had not been considered before."

Jean finished the last of her chocolate cake and continued sipping her coffee. "How do I go about getting these records, John?"

"A letter or a phone call to the Sheriff's Office where the investigation was done could be a logical starting point for the factual side of the case."

"Do you mean there is more?" Jean asked.

"Sure, there is always more. You need to take a close look at motive. Is it reasonable that the wife, what's her name again?"

"Crystal," Jean interjected.

"...that Crystal and Max were desperate enough to take matters into their own hands and carry out a plot such as this? In a very large percentage of homicide cases, there is often a connection to a close family member. If these two were involved with each other, it would be important to know how long they had been carrying on. These things seldom just blossom overnight. Might also be a good idea to consider if Bill had any suspicions. Even though he did have some medical problems, sometimes Alzheimer's patients can see things with an eerie clarity. Maybe he confided his suspicions to a friend or family member who discounted his remarks and just thought he was confused."

"Sounds like a look at the facts is a good beginning, Sir. Why don't we call it a day, and I'll get on my investigative horse again tomorrow. I can't tell you how invaluable your help has been."

"First we're going fishing and then horseback riding? My, my Jean, I didn't know what an outdoorswoman you really were." John teased gently as he placed his arm comfortingly around her shoulders.

Chapter 13
Fortune's Call

After a cursory glance at the Spokesman Review, Jean finished her coffee and began a mental list of the chores she hoped to accomplish before the day was out. She had just determined that the watering could probably wait and that the first order of business should be getting in touch with the Missoula Sheriff's Department when the telephone interrupted her reverie.

"Hello," she greeted the caller cheerily.

"Oh, Jean, I'm so glad you're home," replied the voice at the other end. "I have been dying for news about your trip to Missoula. What did you find out? Did you see Max? What do you think is going on?"

"Whoa, there, Beth. Let's take one topic at a time starting with the subject of YOU. How are you doing? I must admit you sound a bit fragile."

"Well, this has been a difficult pill to swallow...the imagining, the not knowing, the wondering about the future. Please, please, give me some news," Beth pleaded with a noticeable catch in her voice.

Jean had not firmly planned the strategy she would take with Beth, but remembering John's sage advice about just the facts, she decided to take that approach for the time being. "I did see Max and several of the old gang, but I simply don't have any conclusive evidence about 'C,' or how she currently fits into the picture. I do know it was helpful to confront people head on. E-mail and telephone conversations just don't cut it. Speaking of which, why don't you make a trip to Spokane? It would do you a world of good to get away and maybe give you a new perspective on where your future lies." Jean congratulated herself silently for not only skirting the issue, but shifting the conversation away from the real problem at hand...an errant husband and even possible "foul play."

"I simply need more time to piece together my suspicions, the police reports, and the timetable of events," she thought forlornly. Making accusations at this point would be rash and certainly ungrounded.

"The rest of this week is open," Beth replied. "How about if I drive over on Thursday?"

"Perfect," Jean responded, thinking that with some quick footwork she might be able to get reports faxed to her by then. With John's help perhaps she would have some direction by that time. Where oh where were she and her good friend headed, she wondered almost frantically. "I'll plan some fun things to do. Surely shopping, lunch, even a day at the spa will give us a new lease on life."

"A new lease, now there's a thought. My old one seems to have expired with a poof. The kids have been very supportive, although I really hesitate to bad mouth Max; he is, after all, their father, and the past should certainly count for something. On the other hand, some days are a total wash, and I seem to be consumed with undying hatred for the man," Beth confessed angrily.

"Let's go for the positive, Beth. You know our mothers always told us that everything happens for a reason. We just don't know the reason yet. Who knows? Maybe by this time next month we'll have it figured out in spades."

"Right," came Beth's sardonic response. "I'll bring a deck of cards, and if all else fails, we can work on learning to tell our fortunes."

"That's my girl. There's always a way out. Now I'll let you go, so I can start on the plans for the weekend. The fall colors are beautiful.

Maybe I'll plan a little excursion to Green Bluff. We'll pick apples, drink cider, and make the apple dumplings that I know you love so much. "

"OK. It's good to look forward to something. You do promise to give me all the news 'head on,' don't you?"

"Of course, Beth. I'll get my thoughts in order, my ducks in a row, and by the time you get here, we'll figure this thing out in short order. See you Thursday afternoon."

Jean hung up the phone with renewed energy. "OK, OK. We can do this. One step at a time. Since Thursday will be here in three short days, there certainly is no time to waste. I wonder if Fred would help me get some information from the Sheriff's Department or if that would cause speculation and perhaps unwanted gossip. Let's take the objective route; I'll call Missoula and ask for the reports to be faxed. If I can get them today or at least by tomorrow, John and I will have some time to peruse them and see if there are any new interpretations of Bill's untimely end. Thank goodness I decided to buy a printer with a fax. I had no idea it would ever be used for 'detective stuff,' but one never knows, does one?"

A quick call to Missoula information for the telephone number soon linked Jean to a clerk in the Sheriff's office who was very obliging. The clerk explained that the reports were indeed on file and were available for public scrutiny. She would be happy to fax both the police report as well as the autopsy if Jean would give her the fax number and pay for the copies.

"Please send them to 509-664-8976. Also, if you will send me a statement with the copy charges, I'll be glad to send you a check. Thank you so much. You have been more than helpful."

With this task accomplished, Jean felt almost as if a day's work had been finished. Not so. There was still the mail to sort, a quick swish of the dust rag would be good, and she did need a few victuals in the house, especially if Beth was were coming on Thursday. Maybe the pressure would inspire her, and the investigation would finally come to a head.

Chapter 14
Just the Facts, Ma'am

Thursday morning as Jean walked quickly toward her study, she wondered yet again if the autopsy report had come. Yesterday afternoon there had been no word. "What can be taking so long?" she questioned herself. "The police report had come, but she had wanted to have both reports together before she started going over them. "Nuts to that!" she thought. "If the autopsy report is not here today, I'll phone them with my request and start going over the police report."

She started sorting her usual barrage of mail into the usual piles: take care of immediately, go through later, toss immediately. As she was sorting, her fax machine started humming. "Yes!" she thought as she threw the rest of the mail on her desk. As soon as the fax had stopped, she ripped off the sheets, grabbed up the police report along with it and went to the kitchen to get something to drink. She felt a nice cup of Earl Grey tea was appropriate for such an occasion.

As Jean settled into her "reading" chair, she decided to peruse the police report first. It had been hard to wait for the autopsy results, but she was sure the wait would be worth it. She wasn't exactly sure of what she was expecting, but this was much more straightforward than what she had imagined a police report to be. Jean scanned the pages quickly before beginning a more studied approach. As she glanced quickly through the five-page document, she started highlighting things she needed to ask John. First, there were those funny numbers scattered throughout the document. She wondered what they meant. She went into her "English teacher" mode as she had when correcting essays that needed serious deciphering. "Hmmm," she pondered," those numbers are always used as subjects, direct or indirect objects, or objects of the preposition. That must mean they are nouns. Okay, I'll look at some sample sentences to see if I can get a clue. '64-9 was on dam patrol.' 'Called 64-6.' 'Called 65-4 and said didn't need dogs.' Oh, I know what those are, I bet; they must be the officer numbers like those old shows Adam-12 or Car 54, Where Are You? I'll have to check with John to make sure," she thought as she read through the rest of the report.

It was pretty clear what the police had found. A fisherman had called the state police about 11:00 am to report a dead man's body in the water about a mile north of milepost A22. When an officer arrived, he had surveyed the scene, noted the body in the water, and called for the medical examiner and assistance. He had waited for the medical examiner and other policemen before moving the body. They had waded into the river and realized that the body was held partially under the water by some large tree branches that had snagged the man's fishing vest. The body was lying face down in the water. Because the dead man's wallet was evident in his right, back pocket, the officer removed the wallet, opened it, and found the name on the driver's license.

The report also stated that the body was removed from the river and taken to the medical examiner's office. The officer, 64-7, listed the items found on the shore: an insulated thermos; a cooler with several cokes, a partially eaten doughnut, some sort of sandwich, a key ring, and a prescription bottle with what looked like seven capsules still in it. The medical examiner had said that the prescription was for a newer drug for Alzheimer's, but that it would be tested anyway according to procedure. On the shore there were a box for fishing gear, a fishing rod case, a wader belt, and a collapsible chair.

A 1999 GMC Yukon with a Montana plate was on the access road about 500 yards away from the river's edge. The registration in the glove box showed the car was registered to William Pemberton of Missoula, Montana, which matched the information on the driver's license. Officer 64-7 had called his sergeant with the information, so the next of kin could be notified. A tow truck had been called, so the Yukon could be taken to the impound lot.

Officer 64-7 had then gathered all the items found at the scene, put them in his car, and taken them back to the office.

"Well," thought Jean feeling a little ghoulish reading the police report on the death of a friend, "how ironic! All the good things Bill did in his life for others, and his end is just a bunch of facts stated in a no-nonsense manner." Jean remembered what John had told her about looking for the facts and continued with her gruesome task.

Next she had to turn to the autopsy report, something she dreaded doing. "It probably will be in a foreign language. It's a good thing John gave me his copy of Stedman's Medical Dictionary in case I cannot decipher something.

Taking a deep breath, Jean opened the file. She skimmed through the opening information: autopsy number, date of birth, sex, date of autopsy, location, prosecutor, assistant prosecutor, responsible party, etc. Then she came to the meat of the report: the pathological determination of the cause of death which was asphyxia due to fresh water drowning with edema foam in the upper and lower airway. There had been a laceration and some abrasions on the face and forehead, which would have been appropriate for someone falling face first onto the rocks in the water.

As she read through the rest of the report, Jean shook her head. "What had she been thinking to suspect foul play? Obviously, the police knew what they were doing. Well, at least she had looked into it. A knock on her back door brought her back to reality.

She smiled as she saw it was John. He had a bouquet of roses from his garden for her. She opened her back door with a big, welcoming smile. "Hi, are those for me?" He agreed they were and helped her find an appropriate vase. They decided the flowers would look best on the dining room table.

After arranging the vase and flowers just right, they went into the living room. Jean exclaimed,"I received the police and autopsy report, but there is not a thing in there, not one fact, that supports my suspicions! I guess I was being a fool."

John sighed, "Why don't you let me look at the reports to see if there is anything I might notice."

Jean agreed and passed them to him. "Would you like something to drink?" she asked.

"Yes, thanks. Just not that horrible tea you make. How about a soft drink or a glass of water?"

"You bet," Jean responded pleasantly. However, as she entered the kitchen, she mumbled, "Horrible tea, indeed!" She proceeded to get him a glass of water and out of the goodness of her heart, added two ice cubes.

Walking back into the living room, she noticed John frowning. "What's wrong?" she questioned.

He replied," Did you give me all of the autopsy report?"

"Everything I received is in your hands," Jean said. "Why?"

John thought for a moment and then said, "Well, there is no toxicology report, and I find that strange. Every autopsy report includes a toxicology screen. There is even a reference to finding out what was in those capsules in the cooler, but then there is no follow-up. Do you know anything about the medical examiner?"

Jean responded," No, I just know that Hugo Manheim signed the report."

John stared at the report in his hands and finally said, "I think you should ask your friend on the state patrol in Montana about this guy. I don't know for sure, but it seems to me there is something hinky here."

"Hinky. huh?" Jean laughed. "Is that really a word?"

"Well, it is in my vocabulary, and it means something very strange or out of the ordinary," John replied looking almost insulted.

"Okay," Jean laughed again," I'll call Mary Carol and ask her to ask Fred about good ole Hugo Manheim." She was about to bring up something else that she questioned about the report when she heard a car horn tooting in her driveway.

"Oh, oh, I bet that's Beth here from Kalispell. The call to Fred will have to wait until later. Remember Beth's in a world of hurt right now. Be really nice to her, okay?"

John put his arm around her shoulders as they started for the front door and smiled, "I am always nice to beautiful women."

Chapter 15
Is That Crystal Clear?

As Jean and John started out the front door to help Beth gather her things from her car, Jean stopped a moment, turned to John, and told him, "I'm not sure that Beth feels very beautiful right now, John; in fact, she probably feels quite the opposite. I'd like more than anything to help her feel better, so for the next few days I think it's time to put everything else about this investigation into police reports and coroner's reports on the back burner and just concentrate on Beth."

"I think you're right. I'll plan to make myself scarce until after she leaves, and then we can talk more about these other things later."

"Oh, thanks, John!" With that said, Jean sent up a little prayer. "Oh, Dear God, please help!" Then she pasted a smile on her face, and they walked toward Beth, who was emerging from the front seat looking older and more tired than Jean had ever seen her look. She wore gray sweats, and this did nothing for her thin face, which looked almost gray itself. There were hollows around Beth's eyes, which would indicate nights without adequate sleep, and her dishwater-blond hair hung limp to her shoulders. Jean's heart swelled with sympathy for her, and she held out her arms to give Beth a welcoming hug.

Beth glanced at John standing next to Jean, and hesitated for just a moment, then hugged Jean back and said, "I hope it's really okay for me to be here right now, and I'm not interfering with any plans you might have made." She looked apologetically at John and back at Jean.

John extended his hand to Beth, shook her hand warmly, and explained, "I'm John Houck, Jean's neighbor, general handyman, and occasional gardener when she takes a yen to do a little traveling. I just brought some flowers over from my garden so Jean can see how roses really ought to look," he said with an impish grin directed toward Jean. Then he smiled at Beth and added, "I think Jean has been planning some girl stuff for the two of you to be involved in for the next few days, so I'm going to take off and get busy with some of my own plans and leave you two ladies to your own devices.

"Nice to meet you, Beth. I know Jean has been looking forward to your coming to visit. You two try to keep from getting into too much trouble now!" With that, John gave a slight salute to Beth and then Jean and headed for his home.

Beth put her hands on her hips and confronted Jean with "Okay, you better tell me what is going on here. You never mentioned a new man in your life. I don't want to be barging in on your personal life and interrupting any plans the two of you may have made."

"Beth, John and I are friends, and that's it." Jean dropped her eyes momentarily and added with a little smile, "We are becoming better friends, and that's rather nice." She looked back at Beth and went on, "But, believe me, you are not 'barging in' as you put it. I invited you to come, remember, and Beth, I'm so glad you did come," she added with genuine warmth.

Beth gave Jean a second hug and whispered, "Thanks so much for asking me to come." Then she took a step back, smiled slightly and told Jean, "You look great, as usual, and I really appreciate everything you've been doing to help me with this…this…mess in my life." Beth bit her lip, which had begun to tremble slightly, sighed, squared her shoulders, picked up her overnight bag and stated resolutely, "Well! Upward and onward, as they say!"

Taking Beth's cue, Jean reached for the garment bag hanging inside the car and responded with "Right! And now that you're here, the thing we're going to do is look at some things you can do for yourself. We're going to focus on Beth Milner and how to make a good life for her from now on."

"That sounds good, Jean, only I'm not too sure where to begin,"

"Well, I have a few ideas. I just hope I'm not overstepping my boundaries, but seeing Mary Carol put some thoughts into my head. I'll run those by you to see what you think while we relax with a few refreshments."

Minutes later Beth's travel bag was deposited to Jean's guest bedroom, and the two ladies were settled in comfortable chairs on the sun porch with glasses of Chablis and a plate with sliced apple and cheese between them on the small table. Mrs. Robinson lay on her special pillow in the sun.

Beth ran her fingers through her hair absently and asked, "How was your weekend with Mary Carol?"

"It was wonderful to see her again, and she is looking really well," Jean was able to answer quite sincerely. "She has trimmed down a bit, is getting out and walking or running on a regular basis to keep fit, has tinted her hair to get rid of the gray, and she is wearing a bit of make-up, which she hadn't done since Johnny passed away." She had decided it was not the time to make any mention of Fred Williamson being a part of Mary Carol's life, at least not yet.

"I'm glad to hear that. Now what was it about being with Mary Carol that gave you some ideas about a new start for me?"

"This weekend at the Valley Mall there will be several opportunities for both of us to have a free make-over, and then I thought it might be fun to have our hair styled and do a little shopping. You know, typical girl stuff, and just the thing to lift a lady's spirits. What do you think?"

"Sure, why not? What have we got to lose?" Beth looked up and smiled, although Jean sensed it was a bit forced. Frowning slightly, Beth took another sip of Chablis and plunged ahead. "Now for the big question. Did you come to any conclusions about who our infamous 'C' might be?"

"Not conclusively, Beth, and I'm hesitant about making any kinds of guesses or accusations without any real evidence. You know how that is. A man, or woman for that matter, is innocent until proven guilty. I was wondering if you have any ideas yourself."

"I have some ideas and some definite feelings about all of it, of course. In the first place I've wondered if I am to blame myself in some way. Oh, Jean, I have tossed all of this back and forth in my mind so much that it sometimes almost drives me crazy!

"One minute I'm blaming myself for not being a better wife to Max, and the next minute I'd like to invite him over for coffee and lace it with arsenic, and I swear I could actually kill him for what he has done to me and to our family! The kids are so upset with their father that right now they want nothing to do with him, and Andy told me if his dad were to show up right now, he would physically throw him out the door."

Jean remembered Max's questions to her about Beth and his statements about their marriage being a charade, but she kept silent.

"I probably should have been more in tune with Max's wishes to travel, for one thing, and I could have been more willing to move to new areas when his engineering job offered him new and better opportunities. But the kids were young then, and all I could think about was how disruptive this would be to them to pull them out of school and away from their friends. On the other hand, they could have made new friends, and maybe new opportunities would have helped them grow, too. Maybe we would still be a family if I had done that." Tears welled up in Beth's eyes and spilled down her cheeks.

"Beth, dear, that's all water under the bridge now. We don't know how things would be at all if you had been different. Don't beat yourself up over what might or might not have been. I know Max respected you and still does."

Beth looked up quickly. "How do you know that?"

"I had dinner with him one evening while I was in Missoula," Jean responded quietly and carefully. "He asked if I had heard from you and wondered how you are doing."

A sudden light sprang into Beth's eyes. "He did? Do you think there's a chance...I mean, was there anything to indicate that...? Oh, you know what I mean! What do you think, Jean...honestly?

"Quite honestly, Beth, I really don't know, of course, but I wouldn't want to give you any false hope either. Max didn't say anything to indicate his wanting to patch things up."

"Oh." Beth's glance wandered off into the distance and looked sad again. "Well," she sighed, "then 'C' must be the person he really wants." She added vehemently, "Damn her!"

That passionate and uncharacteristic remark startled Jean. This was so unlike the Beth she knew. "You said you had some thoughts yourself about who 'C' might be, Beth. Do you want to tell me what you think?"

"Yes, I do, and then I want to hear your ideas, too. In the e-mail message I intercepted, 'C' seemed to indicate this affair has been going on for some time. Ever since Bill died, Max hasn't been able to do enough for Crystal. She is everything that I am not: passionate, beautiful, daring. At the same time she can seem to be very vulnerable and in need of a man's help. The more I think about it, the more strongly I feel that Crystal Pemberton could be our mysterious 'C'. What do you think?"

Chapter 16
Something in the Wind

Jean gulped awkwardly and barely avoided choking on a bite of cheese. After she recovered and gathered her wits, she did her best to come up with a diplomatic agreement. "Well, Beth, I think you may have hit the nail on the proverbial head. Even though I didn't find any conclusive proof, there seem to be bits and pieces of evidence swarming about that are crying to be assembled into an answer."

"How so?" questioned Beth. "Did Max actually confess? I declare I am going into my arsenic mode right now. Please get on with it!"

Jean wondered almost frantically where to begin. Should she proceed with a chronological order of events, separate the facts and the fantasies, or try to connect the past to the present? "Whoever said life would be easy?" she thought grimly as she took a deep breath and began to pour out her suspicions.

"I guess a good place to start would be my conversation with Max when we had dinner in Missoula. No, he made no 'confession' about anyone, and at first he was rather vehement about discussing 'personal topics.' I did blurt out an inquiry about the possibility of a 'lady-in-waiting,' but this only succeeded in putting him on the defensive; fortunately, I managed to change the subject without too much hostility. He did drink quite a bit during the evening and became quite maudlin about life, and love, and death, as well."

"What on earth are you talking about, Jean?" Beth queried. "How did death enter into the conversation? Surely he isn't contemplating his own end, is he?"

"No, no, certainly not," Jean answered quickly. She squirmed inwardly as she tried to comfort her friend both truthfully and diplomatically. "We talked about the longevity of marriage and how rapidly lives can change. Cases in point were Mary Carol and Crystal who had both lost their husbands unexpectedly,"

"Oh, really. Now the old goat is placing me among the ranks of the widowed? Really, Jean, leaving your wife willingly after 30 years of marriage hardly merits being discussed in the same breath as being involuntarily widowed."

"Just great!" thought Jean with a grimace. "Now I've put her on the defensive. How in the world should I proceed here?" She thought back to John's wise advice, "Just the facts, ma'am, just the facts" and proceeded as straightforwardly and quickly as she could.

"Max seemed to dwell the most on Crystal and Bill. He vacillated between a tearful sorrow about Bill's untimely end and a kind of relief that at last Crystal was free and not burdened with the care of a dependent husband."

Leaving out the references to "beautiful" Crystal, Jean continued. "In spite of this spoken sorrow and concern about the Pembertons, Max behaved rather strangely with Crystal when we all had lunch together. He was cool and aloof, not a bit like Max and his usual bonhomie self. It almost seemed to me as if the 'gentleman doth protest too much.'"

Despite her earlier resolve to set aside her concerns surrounding Bill's death, Jean took a deep breath and plunged ahead with the facts that she could share with Beth. "So with this background in mind and no real proof, a chance encounter at the grocery store really started my mind reeling. Mary Carol and I ran into Nancy Armison at the market. Remember her? Class of '61, cute, curly, and cheerful? She was her usual chatty self and managed to work in some rather unsettling comments about Bill's death."

"Here we go again," Beth interrupted. "This subject again. I'm beginning to get goose bumps."

"Well, just let me bump along to the finish, and we'll see what conclusion you come up with. Maybe my mind has taken a detour and I'm way off base. The remarks Nancy made had to do with how everyone was doing and in particular, how was Crystal, and had they ever figured out exactly what had happened to Bill? She said the investigation regarding his death went on for some time, but the autopsy was inconclusive, and there didn't seem to be any indication of a homicide."

"Homicide—Great Scott! My goose bumps are becoming boulders," Beth shuddered.

"Hang in there, my friend, there's more. Nancy also made some rather inappropriate remarks about Crystal, her art dealings, and her young artist friends."

Beth stifled a giggle and announced, "Well, the 'young' part certainly lets old Max out, now doesn't it?'

"Yes," Jean agreed, "but smokescreens seem to prevail all over the place here. This could certainly be the thickest one of all, especially since I stumbled on Max and Crystal in a rather compromising position on Mary Carol's back porch."

"Ouch!" Beth retorted glumly.

"Let me try to finish. OK? Coupled with Max, his comments and behavior and the strange insinuation of Nancy's, comes a bit of dream lore, fantasy, sub-conscious, I don't really know what to call it," Jean confessed.

"What in the world are you talking about now?" Beth questioned.

"I'm not sure if I have been thinking this thing to death, if I'm going crazy, or if there is something in the wind. Anyway, the night before our get-together at Mary Carol's I had a very troublesome dream—a nightmare if you will."

Hurrying on before Beth's horrified glance could be articulated, Jean continued. "I dreamed that I was drowning in this powerful stream and in spite of my attempts to grab a drifting log, I just couldn't reach the surface. Frantically I groped and struggled, but to no avail, and...and" Jean admitted for the first time, "I felt as if someone were watching me from the shore all the while, but did nothing to help me. Finally, like all bad dreams, this one ended, but my fear is that it didn't end for someone else"

"You mean Bill?" Beth asked in a tremulous voice.

"Maybe. Think about it, Beth. The man, sick or not, was an experienced fisherman. Perhaps he had suspicions about Max and Crystal, perhaps they knew he was on the verge of discovery, perhaps he didn't really drown accidentally."

"What in the world are you implying now? "Beth shrilled.

"I don't know that I'm implying anything at all. I am giving you my conjectures and trying to get your input. It seems strange to me that he didn't have on his wader belt. I also know that the autopsy report contained no indication that a toxicology investigation was performed, and I also know that this should have been a part of the protocol."

"You mean you have pursued the investigation by reading the autopsy? Help! I simply had no idea the whole mess would end up pointed in this direction," Beth protested.

"I told you before I could be on the wrong road or on some stupid detour, but it seems to me since I've come this far, I might as well pursue it till the end."

"You know I'm not being critical, Jean. It's just that it's a lot to assimilate on short notice and on top of everything else. But you know what? It does make me remember a conversation I had with Bill a couple of months before he died."

"Please go on," Jean urged.

"The four of us had dinner together in Kalispell. Bill and Crystal had come for an art show and when she finished we all met at Jaker's. Bill, rather uncharacteristically, drank almost a whole bottle of wine and for some reason when we got to our house, he and I were alone in the kitchen. He had seemed quite reasonable and coherent all evening as we discussed old times, Max's retirement, and Crystal's art show. But all of a sudden, when we were alone, he became agitated. He railed about Crystal and her preoccupation with art and 'God knows what else.' I tried to reassure him that perhaps he felt this way today, but surely tomorrow would be better, thinking that it was only his illness speaking. Maybe I should have clued in on a somewhat corrupted adage, 'From the mouths of husbands.'"

Chapter 17
Relaxation, Refreshment, Renewal, and...?

Jean sighed, "I suppose we could speculate about all of these things from now until who knows how long and still not really know anything for sure. I suggest we just put all of this out of our minds as much as we are able to do, and proceed with our original plans to do our 'girl stuff' and then, as you said earlier, 'upward and onward.' What do you think about that, Beth?"

"I'll go along with that. Personally, I need to get away from the thinking and rethinking of all that's happened lately and work on some kind of attitude adjustment so I don't just come apart at the seams."

"Sounds good. Now then, what is your preference—dinner out tonight or throw something on the barbecue for this evening and eat out tomorrow night?"

"I'd vote for a light supper here tonight, if that's okay with you. More relaxing, I think, and right now that sounds really good to me," Beth responded.

"Actually that sounds best to me, too. Then we can go over a tentative schedule I've been toying with, hit the sack early, and tomorrow we can be up and about and start to work on the new

Beth—and an improved Jean at the same time, complete with make-over's, shopping, hair-do's and whatever."

Friday and Saturday seemed to fly by as the two ladies became caught up in the activities Jean had outlined for them on Thursday evening.

Sunday morning Jean was awakened at 6:30 am by the sound of soft music coming from the clock radio next to her bed. The scent of fresh coffee coming from the automatic coffee maker in the kitchen wafted lazily up the stairs, and as she stretched, Mrs. Robinson, who was curled up by her feet, emitted a soft protest at being disturbed. She became aware of the sound of the shower going in the guest bathroom and knew that Beth was already up.

Jean smiled slightly to herself as she remembered the past two days spent with Beth as they shopped, lunched out, and enjoyed getting made up and having their hair done. With Jean's encouragement Beth had dared to try a new hairstyle and add some color to her usual drab, dishwater blond. Beth, in turn, had urged Jean to go along with the make-up artist's urging to use a darker shade of lipstick and some blush, which brought out the color in her brown eyes and contrasted nicely with her short, thick, salt and pepper hair. Beth had even begun to talk about the future and planned to get her resume in order, so she could go back to work, perhaps even doing volunteer work to add new meaning to her life. "It's true," Jean thought, "sometimes a new look did does help to lift a woman's spirit."

By 8:15 the two women were dressed and in Jean's car on their way to the 8:30 service at the church Jean attended. Beth looked at least five years younger in her new soft blue dress with her cropped and curled hair highlighted with streaks of gold. When they emerged from the church's parking lot, various friends of Jean's from the congregation welcomed Beth enthusiastically as Jean introduced her on their way into the sanctuary. Jean's heart warmed at the sight of Beth's returning smile as she acknowledged the friendly greetings.

Beth was visibly moved at the pastor's message that morning. The sermon was based on the Scripture from the book of Matthew, which read, "Are not two sparrows sold for a penny? Yet not one of them will fall to the ground apart from the will of your Father. And even the very hairs of your head are all numbered. So don't be afraid; you are worth more than many sparrows." After Beth turned to Jean with a tear glistening in her eye and smiled, Jean uttered a silent prayer of thanks.

"Beth," Jean said after church, "how would you feel about packing up a picnic lunch to take with us to Greenbluff when we go to get apples? It's a beautiful day for being outdoors. Then we could make apple cobbler to have with our supper tonight. We'll pick enough so that you can take some fresh, ripe-from-the-tree apples home with you tomorrow. What do you say? Are you in the mood for a picnic and a little apple picking?"

"Yes, I am, Jean! That sounds like just what the doctor ordered."

"Good!" responded Jean, "Besides you know what they say about an apple a day."

Within an hour the two friends had changed into jeans and sweatshirts, had packed some sandwiches, diet soft drinks, and carrot sticks into a small cooler, and were headed into the country for their Sunday afternoon excursion.

It was a beautiful day for a Sunday drive, and they enjoyed the countryside as they left the more densely populated Spokane Valley and drove into the farmland and orchard area known as Greenbluff.

Later the sun warmed their bodies as they picked apples together and filled a small box with them to be weighed and paid for. After their picnic lunch, they decided to save their soft drinks and have some of the fresh apple juice that was for sale, exclaiming over their delicious drinks and savoring every drop.

A short time later Jean and Beth returned to Jean's home, and John Houck, who was in his front yard mowing the lawn, waved to them as they drove into Jean's driveway. When they opened the trunk of the car and started lifting the box of apples, John was beside them before they knew it, lifting the heavy box for them.

As John deposited the apple box on Jean's kitchen counter, it was Beth who told him about the apple dumpling they planned to make for their dessert that night. When she saw John's eyes light up at the mention of apple dumpling, Beth looked at Jean questioningly, and

Jean smiled. "Well, John, I think the least we can do in return for your carting that heavy box in here for us is invite you over to share our Sunday night supper including the apple dumpling."

"I would enjoy that more than I can say," he smiled back. What could I bring to add to the menu?"

"Just yourself."

"How about a bottle of wine?"

"That sounds nice. Would you like to come over about 6:00?"

"Sounds good to me. I'll see you two lovely ladies then."

After enjoying a delicious dinner of pork chops, potatoes, and vegetables, John looked up with an admiring smile for both the ladies as Jean placed a bowl of apple dumpling swimming in cream on the table before him. "This little visit together seems to have been good for both you ladies," he commented rather casually. "You both look…well, healthier and bright-eyed somehow. I can't quite put my finger on it, but both of you do look pretty darned good! Boy! And so does this apple dumpling!" He added appreciatively after they each had a bowl of dessert before them.

Beth noted a slight flush to Jean's cheeks as she responded with, "Thank you very kindly, Sir," which brought a wistful smile to Beth's face.

Beth turned to John and told him, "Jean is a wonderful friend to have, and I am so grateful to her for all she's done for me. I…well…I've been dealing with some problems in my life lately, and she has been helping me with all of it. The past few days are a part of that assistance, and believe me," and turning to smile at Jean, "they have helped!"

Jean smiled back at Beth and said, "It's been marvelous having you here, Beth, and I've enjoyed every moment of it!" She added half apologetically, "I hope you don't mind that I have confided some of the problems to John. When I was having doubts about some of my thoughts and wondering what to do next, I sort of unloaded them on him. He's the one who advised me to just stick with the facts and helped me to formulate a plan to get the reports from the authorities regarding Bill's death.

"It's okay, "Beth reassured Jean. "I know you would tell these things to someone only to find a way to help, not just to indulge in idle gossip."

"From what I'm learning about your friend Jean here, she doesn't appear to be as gossipy as most women, so I think your trust is well-founded," John said to Beth. "Of course, I could be wrong, too. I'll just have to get to know her better and wait and see." His eyes twinkled as he grinned at Jean when he made this last remark.

Jean's eyes met his, and this time a full-fledged blush crept from her neck to her ears to the top of her hairline.

John cleared his throat slightly and continued, "Let's see, where were we now? We were talking about Beth and problems, and then I think you mentioned something about your friend Bill and some doubts connected with his decease. There is one thing that concerns me in that respect as well," John said thoughtfully, changing the subject abruptly. He put both his hands behind his head and leaned back in his chair, "and that is the fact that the coroner did not include a toxicology report. Now this may not mean a thing, but it just makes me wonder what kind of coroner he is by neglecting to do this very routine piece of work."

"I'll plan to call Mary Carol tomorrow and see what I can learn about Dr. Manheim soon to set your mind at ease then."

John smiled slightly, "An easy mind will be only temporary, I'm sure, until you come up with who knows what! No, no! Don't hit me! Don't hit me!" He threw his hands up in mock protest as Jean picked up her now empty dessert bowl.

"Don't be so paranoid. I'm just clearing off the table," she smiled sweetly.

"If you two will promise not to beat each other up too badly, I'm going to excuse myself and start packing," Beth said as she stood up. "I want to hit the road early tomorrow, so I can have a leisurely drive back to Kalispell and maybe stop a few times on the way, too. You know what? Packing is going to take a little more planning with the new things I bought."

"Don't worry, Beth. Jean will be safe, and so will I. To insure the latter I'm going to head home myself, and you two can have a little time left to yourselves before you leave in the morning. It was very nice meeting you, Beth, and I wish you the very best. I know something about the difficulty of a marriage ending myself. It's not easy, but life does go on, and, who knows? It may be even better than before. I hope that's the case for you." With that, John gave Beth's shoulder a slight squeeze and turned to Jean. "Thanks for a very good dinner and for inviting me over. I'd offer to help with dishes, but I figure the dishwasher will take care of that. I'll see you tomorrow sometime." He gave her shoulder a pat and was gone.

Chapter 18
Questions, Questions, Questions

As Jean waved goodbye to the retreating car, she hoped Beth would continue to do better. Jean felt the time she and Beth had had together over the past few days had been well spent. "Well, I'll just have to make sure I keep in close contact with her and make sure she keeps this positive attitude," she mused as she walked back into the house.

"Okay, what's on the agenda for today? Oh, it's still early enough I could call Mary Carol before she goes off to work." She got a cup of tea from the kitchen, her address book from her desk, and settled herself comfortably into her reading chair. Before she dialed, she looked out her front window and smiled. She truly loved living across from an elementary school. If the weather were good, the children gathered early in the morning to begin their play. Today was no exception. The swings were full as was the slide. Several young girls were playing hopscotch. Jean wrested her gaze away from the window and turned to the task at hand.

The phone rang once, twice, and then she heard, " Hello? Hang on a minute." There was a clank, a muttering, and then once again, "Hello."

"Mary Carol, what is going on?" Jean asked.

"Oh, Jean, I was trying to balance my yogurt, banana, and a cup of coffee as well as napkins when I answered the phone. Sorry," Mary Carol replied.

"No problem. I just wanted to make sure everything was all right," Jean said. "How are you doing?"

"I am absolutely fantastic. How about yourself?" Mary Carol answered.

"I am fine. Beth just left. We had a good time together, did some great shopping, had some terrific conversations, and she even got a makeover. Wait 'til you see her," Jean confided.

"Oh, I am so glad. I have really been worried about her. She has seemed so sad and reticent since the split. I tried to call her a couple of times, but she never wanted to talk. It was always short and to the point," Mary Carol replied, the concern evident in her voice.

Jean said, "I am sure she is going to do better from now on. I think we should both call her every once in a while and make sure she stays on the road to recovery."

Mary Carol said hurriedly, "Sounds good to me. I hate to rush you, but I am running a little late today. What can I do for you?"

Jean hesitated for a moment and then said, "Well, my book group has assigned me the task of coming up with some information about a coroner's report. Since I convinced them to set the story in Missoula, they thought it would only be fair if I were the one to obtain the information.

"I vaguely remember the name Hugo Manheim as coroner from reading the paper while I was visiting you. Do you know if I got the coroner's name right, or could you possibly give me his name and address?" Jean asked.

"Hugo Manheim? I never heard of him. Why do you need the name and address of the coroner, for heaven's sake?" Mary Carol questioned.

"Well, I have to get a copy…" Jean started to reply when she heard a female voice in the background and heard Mary Carol say, "Oh, Crystal, you have to go? Okay, I'll call you back after I get home this evening, and we can plan that. Bye."

"Sorry about that," Mary Carol said as she came back on the line. "Crystal was here talking to me about a community dinner; we are in charge of the decorations. I'm sorry we interrupted you."

"Oh, that's okay. Anyway, as I was saying, I have to get a copy of a coroner's report on a poisoning that will fit the mystery we are writing," Jean stated.

Mary Carol answered, "I understand now, but why not just ask Fred if he can get you one?"

Jean replied, "Do you think he would help out? I guess I could do that, thanks. Do you have his number?"

"Are you kidding?" Mary Carol answered laughing. "I have it memorized. It's 555-1418. Don't call him before nine tonight though because he's on duty all day."

"Thanks so much. I'd better let you eat your breakfast and get off to work. Have a good one," Jean wished Mary Carol, said goodbye, and hung up.

Jean sat in her chair and thought it had been easier than she thought it would be to get Fred's number from Mary Carol. However, it might be difficult to fool Fred about why she needed the information. Maybe she had better tell the truth and be prepared for the lecture about snooping that probably would follow. She had much to do during the day including writing an outline for her next chapter in the "group" book for the Friday meeting, so she had better get to work!

Later that evening after watching a rerun on TV once again, she noted it was time to give Deputy Fred a call. She dialed carefully and waited.

"Deputy Williamson," a deep voice answered.

"Hi, Fred. It's Jean Smiley in Spokane. How are you?"

" Hi, Jean. I'm fine but a little surprised to hear from you," he responded hesitantly.

Jean thought to herself and chuckled, "Maybe he thinks I'll question him about Mary Carol."

Before she could say anything, however, he said quickly, "Is everything all right?"

She laughed and said, "Yes, I just called to ask you a question or two. I have been thinking about Bill's Pemberton's death ever since I came home from Missoula. I just keep thinking things are not quite right, and I need to set my mind to rest." There was silence on the other end of the line, so she just rushed onward.

"I ordered the coroner's report on Bill's death. It was signed by a Hugo Manheim. What do you think of him? Also, there was no toxicology screen included as part of the report. Is that normal?"

"Well," Fred began slowly, "first of all, I guess I should not be surprised about your interest or even that you have the coroner's report. If I remember correctly from high school, you were always the one to try to set things right and always interested in things that many felt were not your business."

Jean didn't know quite what to say, but before she could respond, Fred continued, "Hugo Manheim is the assistant coroner. He only fills in when our regular guy, Dr. Robert South, is away from the county or on vacation. As for how I feel about him, I try not to think of him at all."

Jean laughed but pursued the point, " Okay, Wise Guy. What is your professional opinion of the man?"

"I do not think much of the man personally or professionally. He takes too many short cuts and is just plain lazy. As to your other question, there should be a toxicology screen on all questionable deaths. However, I did talk to Hugo about this one. He claimed it was obvious how Bill died and did not want to distress the widow any more. Apparently he has been a good friend of the family for several years."

"Really?" Jean interjected.

Fred continued, "Between you and me, I think it was a case of shoddy work, as usual, but I think he may have been right about there being no question of how Bill died. Because there was no evidence pointing to the contrary, there was no reason to pursue anything further…at least as far as my captain was concerned."

"Did you think it should have been pursued?" Jean questioned as Mrs. Robinson rubbed against her legs.

YVONNE DEITZ, VIKKI MOORMANN, SUSAN SCHREIBER

"Well, yes. I thought Manheim should have done a toxicology screen on the body, pills, and contents of the thermos as per regulations and called him to ask if he had taken the required tissue sample. He had. But my captain said there was no point to the test because of the cost to the county, so that was the end of that.'

"Any more questions?" Fred asked.

"No, I guess that's all. I really appreciate the help. I just cannot help thinking Bill's death may not have been accidental," Jean replied.

"Can you give me any concrete reasons why?" Fred questioned with a definite note of interest in his voice.

"Not yet," she said, "but when I do I'll give you a call."

Mrs. Robinson meowed in agreement.

Chapter 19
Truth or Fiction?

Tuesday morning Jean awakened to the sound of rain falling on her patio roof. Mrs. Robinson uttered a loud protest as Jean sat up and slid her feet into the slippers beside her bed. "I'd better make sure I didn't leave any windows open anywhere else," she muttered to herself as she closed her bedroom window, which had been open a crack, and mopped up the small amount of moisture on the windowsill with a tissue.

Mrs. Robinson meowed again as she followed Jean from room to room. "Well, now, Mrs. R., what are you so upset about? It's time for us to be up and about anyway, and you don't need to be so impatient either. Your breakfast will be in your dish in just a minute."

Just then the phone rang. "Who would be calling this early in the morning? It's only 8:00 o'clock."

"Meow!" was Mrs. Robinson's response.

"You don't say."

"Hello," Jean spoke into the phone.

"Hello, Jean. I hope I didn't wake you up. I just realized you're in a different time zone, and it's an hour earlier there than it is in Missoula," a somewhat familiar voice said from the other end of the line.

"Crystal? Is that you?" Surprised that Crystal would be calling her, Jean asked, "What's up? Is everything all right over there?"

From the corner of her eye she could see Mrs. Robinson staring intently at the phone. The hair on her back seemed to be standing on end.

"Things could not be better," Crystal replied almost too enthusiastically. "It just so happens that I will be in your area day after tomorrow to meet with a young artist to plan a showing of his work the end of this month. We will be meeting in the morning and then later in the afternoon as well, and I thought you and I might have lunch together if you are available. I have about an hour and a half right around noon that is currently free. I was wondering if you would like to drive into Spokane and meet me at the Davenport Hotel where my meeting is. It could be like old times. What do you say? I hope your answer is 'Yes,'" Crystal added.

Jean was momentarily taken aback since it really was not like old times at all. She and Crystal never were very close even in high school. Crystal had been a cheerleader, and Jean was on the school newspaper and yearbook staffs. About the only things they had in common were their friendships with Bill Pemberton, and those were of a completely different nature, and the fact that Jean had dated Bill's older brother for a while, and the two couples double-dated a few times.

"Well, um, sure, Crystal, I'd be glad to meet you for lunch at the Davenport. What time shall we meet and exactly where?"

"I'm so glad you can do this, Jean!" Crystal gushed. "Shall we say 12:30 in the lobby near the fountain?"

"That will be just fine, Crystal. Thursday at 12:30 in the Davenport lobby near the fountain. I'm writing it on my calendar."

"Wonderful! I'll see you then. Bye." Crystal hung up.

"This is very interesting," Jean thought to herself. "I think this is the first time Crystal has ever called me to arrange a meeting with her. What on earth...? I wonder if this has anything to do with her overhearing part of my conversation with Mary Carol yesterday. I wonder if Fred said anything to Mary Carol about his conversation with me, and then I wonder if Crystal got wind of any of my investigating. Oh, wow! What have I gotten myself into here?" She uttered her exclamation and last question out loud, to which Mrs. Robinson responded with another loud and rather disgusted "Meow!"

"Mrs. R., I would swear you can understand every word I say!" At that point Mrs. Robinson began to wash her face nonchalantly. "Excuse me, Missy; you don't need to be so smug about it." Jean bent down and rubbed her feline friend's chin and was rewarded with a loud purring sound. "You do have a nice motor, though, even if you are a bit conceited at times."

As Jean picked up the cat's dish to rinse it out and refill it, she thought, "I wonder what John's thoughts would be about this sudden desire of Crystal's to get together with me for lunch. I'm tempted to call and tell him about it, but, on the other hand, I don't want to make a pest of myself either. After all, it may not mean anything at all. Guess I'd better wait and see."

Wednesday came and went, and Thursday dawned as another gray, drizzly day. As Jean glanced out her kitchen window while she finished washing her few breakfast dishes, she considered, "The fall rains have started. Won't be long and the trees will be losing their leaves. Oh, well," she sighed slightly, "such is life: one season followed by another. I remember learning in my intro to philosophy class in college that the only thing constant is change. How true that is! Not all change is bad, though. Don't let yourself turn into a little old lady who balks at changes in her life." Then she remembered John's words to Beth on Sunday evening when he told her almost the same thing about change and how her life just might get better than it ever was. She smiled at that and uttered a little prayer of thanks for her neighbor who was becoming a rather good and special friend to her, better than she had thought might be possible. Smiling at that and at a streak of sunlight breaking through the clouds momentarily, she took that as a good omen, hung her dishtowel over a rod under her kitchen sink, and moved toward her bedroom to get dressed for her lunch with Crystal at the Davenport Hotel.

At 12:30 Jean sat in one of the quietly elegant, velvet, upholstered arm chairs in the hotel lobby admiring the beautiful surroundings and trying to feel more comfortable about the impending meeting with Crystal when that lady entered.

Crystal was wearing a soft rose raincoat, which contrasted beautifully with her long, dark hair, and she carried an umbrella of the same color and fabric.

Several gentlemen gave her admiring glances as she swooped to where Jean was waiting. "Jean, dear," she said, "I'm so glad you could make it! I've made reservations for us in the Palm Court Restaurant, so they should be ready for us now. My, but you are looking fit!" This last comment succeeded in giving Jean the feeling that she was years older than Crystal and was fortunate to be in good health. Jean rose, and the two women began walking toward the Palm Court.

"Thank you, Crystal, I am, as you put it, quite fit, and you look well, too, I'm happy to say. Aren't we the lucky ones, though?" Jean smiled disarmingly, and Crystal was momentarily speechless, but only momentarily.

"Indeed, we are fortunate, Jean, in many ways. I can hardly wait to tell you about the charming young artist I am working with today. You must look at the work he is going to have on exhibit next month right here in the Davenport! They are going to give us an area on the mezzanine, and there will be a reception so that other art lovers will be able to meet this young protégé of mine, and of course, I will be here with him as well. I could send you an invitation if you will come, and if you would like to bring a friend, I can arrange for that, too.

"Thank you, Crystal, I just may take you up on that." Jean smiled again wondering if John might be persuaded to accompany her to what she felt might be some kind of artsy circus. It could be rather interesting.

They reached the restaurant, and a young woman showed them to their table, which was gracefully appointed with a white tablecloth, pastel napkins, fine silver and a pink rosebud in a silver vase.

As Jean perused the menu, Crystal remarked, "Mmmm, chocolate silk pie for dessert sounds excellent!"

Jean laughed, "Crystal, you amaze me. I see that hasn't changed since we were in school together. You still think about dessert first. Now most of us have to be careful about that sort of thing, or just thinking about sweets too much seems to put weight on the hips. Yet here you are planning on dessert, and you still maintain the same svelte figure. How do you do it?"

Crystal smiled appreciatively. "I really do watch what I eat most of the time, and I work out on a regular basis as well. I always have. Probably a habit I developed when I was a cheerleader, and it has just stayed with me.

After the waitress had taken their orders and their menus, Crystal leaned forward in her chair slightly and said to Jean, "I can't begin to tell you how excited I am about Greg Applebee, the young artist I am working with today. He has done some wonderful paintings of scenes here in the Pacific Northwest, which will no doubt help to put the area on the map of the entire art world. We could have artists coming from all over the world to our own back door after they see some of his stunning scenes and realize what fabulous beauty we have to offer to artists in various media. It could become an artists' paradise!"

"I've always felt we live in one of the most beautiful areas of the world," Jean observed quietly. "I'm not sure I would want it to become much more known for that than it already is, though. So many people are moving into not just this area, but I'm sure you've seen the same thing happening in western Montana, too. Houses are springing up everywhere, farmland is being grabbed up by land developers, traffic is increasing, and so is the crime rate as the population increases."

"Now, Jean, don't become one of those old-fashioned people who balk at progress of any kind. If the area becomes an artists' paradise, as I've mentioned, I believe the segment of people who want certain areas set aside for preservation from development will increase. Artists are a special breed!" Crystal became rather emotional as she uttered her last statement.

Jean did not want to get into any kind of debate with Crystal, so she changed the subject slightly by asking, "You said you could get me an invitation to this showing of your artist's work. I'd like to see what he has done, and I think I'd like to bring someone along. By the way, what did you say his name is, and how old is he?"

"His name is Greg Applebee, and he is twenty-seven years old. He's been out of art school for five years now and has been earning a meager living free-lancing, but he needs some major exposure to really get what he deserves for his work, and I am prepared to help him achieve that." Crystal was appeased by Jean's request and seeming interest in Greg's work. "I'll see that you get an invitation as soon as I get home in a couple of days. I'm glad you plan to bring a friend, too. Anyone I know?" she asked curiously.

"Thanks, Crystal. I thought I would ask a neighbor of mine. No one you know."

The server brought their food then, and to Jean's relief the two women became absorbed with eating.

After a few moments of silence, Crystal looked up at Jean and said in a rather off-hand manner, "Well, now, Jean, tell me what you have been up to since you retired from teaching. I think I heard something about a book you were writing with some friends. Does it have anything to do with schools or teaching or anything else that might be in your combined areas of expertise?"

"Actually, no, it has nothing to do with school or anything remotely related to teaching. The three of us used to be involved in writing English curriculum on various curriculum committees over the years, and we had a good time doing that together. We all enjoy reading, as might be expected, and we all enjoy reading mysteries. One day as we were having lunch together we came up with the idea of writing a mystery novel together, so that's what we're doing. We are having a great time doing it!"

"Well, tell me about your book. What kind of mystery is it, and where is it set?"

Jean finished her cup of soup, set it aside, and said, "We're writing a murder mystery, and since we are all familiar with this part of the country, we've set it in the Northwest, western Montana, to be specific."

Crystal put down her fork. "How interesting!" she said thoughtfully.

This came as a bit of a surprise to Jean, since Crystal had never shown a particular interest in anything Jean did before.

"Tell me some of the specifics," Crystal said, folding her arms on the table and looking at Jean with undivided attention.

Jean swallowed and decided to plunge right in and see what kind of reaction she might get from Crystal. "It deals with infidelity in a marriage that everyone thought was practically perfect, and the result is death. A wife murders her husband."

"Because the husband was unfaithful?" Crystal asked.

"No, because the wife was unfaithful, and she wanted to get her husband out of the way."

"Well, well," Crystal responded rather slowly. "Since you've just given away the plot, I guess I won't need to buy the book." She looked at her watch and pushed her chair back. "Oh, dear, the time has just flown by, and I must rush off to meet Greg. So sorry to hurry away like this, but I really must go!" With that, Crystal picked up her things and left, leaving Jean to pay the bill.

Chapter 20
Strangers in the Night

As Jean lay in her bed, her mind tossed and turned. First, she could not get over the bizarre lunch she had had with Crystal. At first Crystal had been oh, so friendly, something she had never been before. Then suddenly she had left abruptly quite a while before the hour and a half Crystal had said she had free...even without having dessert! Everyone who knew Crystal knew she always had dessert. What was going on with that woman? Jean's uneasy feelings about Crystal magnified as the night progressed, and she tried to rid her mind of such thinking. Maybe she was just irritated because Crystal had stuck her with the check.

Jean knew she would never get to sleep if she did not quit thinking about Crystal. She had to think of something more pleasant. "Oh, I know. I'll think about having breakfast with John," she mused. She had been amazed at how, when not hearing from him for a couple of days, she had really missed him. When he had called last night to invite her to breakfast for his famous ham and cheese omelets, she had been so happy. "I really enjoy spending time with him," she smiled to herself. Still smiling, she finally fell asleep.

Suddenly a jarring sound ripped her from a sound sleep and a very romantic dream. Mrs. Robinson was venting her frustration also from the bottom of the bed. Flicking on the bedside lamp, she glanced at the clock as she reached for the phone. "Oh, no," she thought," it must be trouble if someone is calling at 4:00 am in the morning. "Hello?" she answered hurriedly. At first there was no sound on the other end of the line. She said, "Hello?" once again. Still no reply, but then she could hear breathing.

A deep voice then threatened," Butt out of other people's business, or you will be sorry!"

Jean could not believe what she was hearing. "Who is this?" she demanded. There was no answer; in fact the line was dead. The whole episode really bothered Jean. Even though she had lived alone most of her adult life and thought she was pretty darned independent, something happening like this made her spine crawl. She knew she would never go back to sleep now, so she had better get up and do something useful with her time, something like cleaning the oven, a task she truly despised.

Three hours later her oven, as well as the whole kitchen, was spotless. She even had made some cinnamon rolls in her bread machine to take over to John's for breakfast. She looked at the kitchen clock and grimaced, "Just enough time to shower and change my clothes," she thought as she rushed upstairs to her bathroom.

After her shower she gazed into her mirror and sighed, "I look like the wreck of the Hesperus. Oh, well, I'll just have to make the best of it. Maybe my warm cinnamon rolls will distract John's attention from my drawn face and droopy hair." Jean dressed quickly in her newest navy blue, silk, sweat suit, put on her socks and tennis shoes, and went downstairs to gather the rolls.

As she crossed the yard and entered John's through the side gate, she put on what she hoped was a convincing smile. After all, she was mighty glad to see him!

John had seen her coming and opened the door for her with a very welcoming smile," Hi, I'm so glad you could join me this morning. Are you all right? You look awfully tired...or something?" he asked wonderingly.

Jean smiled sincerely at his concern and responded," Yes, I am fine. I just did not get much sleep last night. I had an annoying crank call around 4:00 this morning." She paused for a minute and then continued, "Then I could not get back to sleep, so I got up and cleaned my oven."

"But you hate cleaning your oven," John said. "The call must have really upset you." He came around to her side and put his arm around her. His arm was warm and comforting.

Jean replied, "Well, it's not often I have someone call me at that time of the morning to tell me in a threatening tone that I had better butt out of other people's business."

"Was it a man or a woman? Did he or she say anything else?" John questioned seriously.

"It was a man, a younger man I think. When I started to ask who was calling, the line went dead," Jean answered.

"I do not like this!" John said loudly. "I know you are always interested in other people and the things that happen to them, but what do you think precipitated the call?"

Jean backed away and frowned, "I thought I was coming over here for breakfast, not the inquisition."

John said apologetically, "I am so sorry. I just have to finish cutting up the fruit and start the omelets." He started to walk toward the refrigerator, then turned and said, "You know I just care about you, don't you?"

"Yes, I know, but I am so tired now. I just need some friendship and good food," Jean responded.

"Okay, you've got both right here and even some TLC...you know, tender loving care," John smiled.

"Yes, I know, and I appreciate all of it, really!" Jean answered, smiling.

John responded, "Then let's get on with breakfast, and we can talk afterward if you want."

"Sounds good to me," Jean said as she turned toward the slicing board and the waiting cantaloupe.

After an absolutely delicious breakfast, they moved into the front room with their coffee and tea. Jean marveled that this man was such a good cook, incredible gardener, neat housekeeper, intelligent, witty companion, and even better was such a delicious hunk. She shook her head at her fanciful mental meanderings.

"What?" John questioned.

"Nothing," Jean said and shook her head to reinforce the notion, even though she could feel her cheeks warming.

"Okay," John asked," what have you been up to in the last day or two that has been interesting?"

"I received a surprising telephone call from Crystal. You remember my talking about Crystal, don't you? Absolutely gorgeous, Bill's wife?" Jean remarked. "She never has had much time for me or interest either, but suddenly Tuesday morning she called. She said she was in town meeting with one of her young artists and thought it would be nice if we could have lunch Thursday. I was so floored I had to say yes. She suggested we meet at the Davenport, which was where she was staying, in the lobby at 12:30."

"Why do you think she is so interested in you all of a sudden?" John asked.

"I don't know. Maybe since Bill is gone, she realizes she needs all the friends she can get. The thing is, it was a pretty strange lunch." Jean stated frowning.

"What was strange about it?" John inquired.

"Crystal said she had heard from Mary Carol about the book I am writing with two other retired English teachers, and then she wanted to know about the book. I gave her a bit of a song and dance about a marriage with infidelity and then said that, of course, the wife had murdered her husband. That was when things really got tense at the table. She suddenly decided she had to leave, and then she did, and without having dessert!"

"Why was the fact that she did not have dessert so important?" queried John.

"Because anyone who knows Crystal at all knows she always has dessert. In fact she usually picks out her dessert before she orders her lunch or dinner. She is this petite size four and always has desserts and never gains an ounce," Jean answered with a disgusted look on her face.

"And that was the last you saw her or heard from her?" asked John.

"Yes. Do you think that strange call this morning might have been related to what I said?" Jean asked John.

"I really don't know at this point, but I do think it is suspicious. I also think you have reached a point where you need to tell, what's his name—Fred of your suspicions and then see what happens," John stated rather firmly.

"Okay, you may be right; I will call Fred this evening," Jean replied.

"No," John rejoined," I think you need to go to Missoula and see him in person. In fact, I will go with you to offer support. Plus, I want to hear personally what Fred says."

Surprised, Jean said, "Are you sure that is necessary?"

John answered solemnly, "Yes. When do you want to go? I am free all this week."

Jean answered slowly, "Actually tomorrow would be the best time to go as I am free for the next two days. Then I have to be back for an eye appointment."

"That would be fine with me. Do you want to make the arrangements, or should I?" John countered.

"Why don't you do it? I am so tired I probably would make them for next August. In fact I think I am going home now to take a good nap before I start making my own arrangements for Mrs. Robinson and packing. What time do you want to leave tomorrow?" Jean asked.

"How about 7:00?" John questioned.

"That sounds good. I'll see you then." Jean paused, "You know, I think I feel good about going, like I am taking control again."

"John laughed, "I know; you are such a controlling woman," and gave her another warm hug and a peck on the cheek.

Chapter 21
Mischief in Missoula

Traveling with John promised to be amusing at the very least. Arriving at Jean's back door at the stroke of 7:00, he was rarin' to go and could not even be persuaded to have a cup of coffee. "The sooner we get on the road, the sooner we get down the road," he promised in a very Yogi Berra-like manner.

Fortunately, the night before Jean had packed the few essentials she needed for an overnight stay, and it was simply a matter of tossing her suitcase in the back of John's green and clean Durango. Mrs. Robinson had food and water for a couple of days, and Jean bade her a hasty good-bye as she closed the front door.

The first miles of the trip were comfortably silent perhaps because of the lack of caffeine. Jean thought briefly about pleading for a stop for coffee in Coeur d'Alene, but thought better of it as they sped down the freeway. She gazed contentedly out the window and mulled over the turn of events since last she had made this trip. "Actually," Jean chided herself," it might be better to think about something else entirely. Maybe it would will clear my head when we talk to Fred."

Finally Mr. Companionable, Caffeine-free, Chauffeur broke the silence. "I've thought a bit about this case and tried to dredge up anything similar to it that I worked on in California. Several cases come to mind in which the widow was a rather clever perpetrator. One case involved poison, which was administered in increasingly lethal doses in the form of vitamins. Turns out mama was seeing a pharmacist who promised that the poison would never be detected. What a bitter pill to swallow when she found out he had promised more than he could deliver."

"Was an autopsy performed then? Jean queried.

"Actually not until some time later when the widow's kids became suspicious that Mama and the druggist became a little too friendly, a little too soon. After the body was exhumed, traces of the poison were found in the poor health-conscious husband who had merely been trying to stay healthy by taking his vitamins. The rest, of course, was easy. Who had access to the medicine cabinet? Who might have tampered with the contents? Who had a motive to see the demise of "Mr. Good Health"? I've told you before that 90% of the homicide cases investigated can be routed back to a close family member."

"I know, John, but it is just damn difficult to think of an old friend in the role of a murderess or as someone who would threaten me. Not that Crystal and I have ever been "bosom buddies," but we do certainly have a history that goes back to the time we were kids."

"Maybe murderers are made not born. How much do we know about the trauma of living with an Alzheimer's victim? How much do we know about the temptations offered by someone with vitality, good looks, and charm?"

Jean smiled secretly to herself as she glanced quickly at John. His distinguished profile, steel gray hair, and clean-cut good looks might have provided an answer to that very question. Not knowing exactly how to segue into a comparison between Max and John, she turned her gaze to the front window and decided to change the subject.

"Tell me about the most interesting case you ever worked on, "Jean asked.

"Well, there was a rather grim one where the husband was a contractor and managed to cement his relationship with his nagging wife by enclosing her in the foundation of a bridge. The woman simply disappeared without a trace until an earthquake moved the abutment a few feet to reveal her remains."

"Ugh, let's talk about something more uplifting."

"There's always the case of the airplane pilot who tampered with the parachute of his dearly beloved."

"Not that kind of uplifting, you goose. When do we get to stop for something to eat?"

After a welcome break fortified with coffee and toast, John suggested that Jean wait to try to catch Fred Williamson at home after work, a tactic that would preclude anyone's overhearing their conversation or really even knowing that they were in Missoula.

"Indeed, we do need to slip in and out of town as quickly and quietly as possible. Let's keep our fingers crossed that Max and Crystal don't make an unwelcome and unexpected appearance. I'd also like to avoid Mary Carol this one time as well. The fewer people who speculate about our interest in the investigation, the better off we'll be. I just hope we haven't made a mistake by not calling ahead to tell Fred we were coming," Jean fretted.

"Ah, but look at it this way, "John smiled. "We've had several hours of a profitable conversation and the promise of a leisurely dinner. You know that something good always comes from everything."

"You are the quintessential optimist, John, and I must say you are a good sport, too."

After a leisurely lunch and stroll along the river bank, the detective duo checked into Jean's favorite hotel, the Doubletree. The adjacent rooms on the riverside promised to offer a quiet retreat after they had talked to Fred.

Jean suggested they take some time to settle in and maybe even catch a quick nap. Then they agreed to meet in the bar about 4 o'clock, and from there they wwould make arrangements to meet Fred.

Jean dozed off briefly and awoke in time to watch Oprah, which inspired her with renewed energy and a determination to answer unresolved questions. After a quick slap of lipstick, a hurried brush of her hair, and a hasty glance through the Missoula phone book, Jean gathered her purse and key and made her way downstairs to find John observing a fisherman on the banks of the river. "I've ordered a gin and tonic. What's your preference, Jean?"

"Sounds perfectly refreshing to me. After we order, let's use your cell to call Fred at the office. If we can snag him there, maybe we can forestall any other plans he might have for this evening. Also, it might give him a chance to review the records on this case."

"Your wish is my command, Jean Queen. Do you want to make the call, or shall I?"

"Well, John, it might lend a bit of authority if you called. Of course, you need to tell him that we are here together because my name would add a bit of familiarity, don't you think?"

The timing of the visit as well as the phone call proved to be fortuitous. Fred agreed to see them about 8:30 after his shift was over. He gave directions to his home on the east side of town and seemed genuinely interested in the brief amount of information that John gave him.

Dinner provided a welcome respite from the drive, the strategy, and the worry. Jean relaxed and enjoyed herself and the light conversation she always managed with John. It seemed as if they, like her Missoula counterparts, had been friends for a long, long time. Strange, wasn't it that this foray into the possibility of a murder could result in a developing friendship with a neighbor? Well, who was it who had said earlier, 'something good comes from everything?'" Fred's directions, and of course, Jean's familiarity with Missoula made short work of finding his east side rambler. Fred greeted them warmly and invited them to join him on the back deck where he was just cooling off with a frosty beer. Jean introduced John, his background, and his interest in helping her with the case. Then after declining his offer to join him for a drink, Jean decided to come straight to the point.

"We're here, Fred, for several reasons. When I was here several weeks ago, I ran into Nancy Armison who suggested that Bill Permberton's death had been investigated as a homicide. Apparently nothing came of that investigation, but somehow that suggestion caused the hair on the back of my neck to stand up. You probably know that Beth and Max Milner have split up and that Max has been quite chummy with Crystal Pemberton. I'm sure you remember seeing them together at Mary Carol's. It just seems to me that both of them have an untoward attitude about Bill: Max seems to be excessively maudlin, and Crystal is, oh, I don't know, sharp somehow," Jean offered.

John picked up the thread of Jean's concern and explained, "When Jean first shared her suspicions and concerns with me, I suggested that she get to the heart of the matter by looking at the facts. That resulted in her request for an autopsy report, which proved little, except I did notice there was no toxicology report. She then spoke with you on the phone about that and about the reliability of the assistant coroner, Hugo Manheim. I think the two of you spoke about that, and we appreciated your assessment of Manheim's ability and work ethic. The long and short of that conversation led you to a legitimate question 'Do you have any concrete evidence that may point to a suspect?'"

"Actually, at that point, we had only our suspicions," Jean continued. 'However, since then I have received a rather threatening phone call which suggested that I butt out of matters that don't concern me and mind my own business. I can't help but think there is a connection to my inquiries about Bill's death."

"Who knows about your amateur investigation?" Fred asked drolly.

"Beth Milner does. Of course, she has a vested interest because of Max. And then there is Mary Carol, I suppose, since I called her to get your telephone number. I was a bit circular when I told her the reason I needed it, though. Told her I was writing a mystery and needed access to an autopsy report. I know that you two are good friends, and I hope you'll keep her out of this. She doesn't even know we're here for a quick visit. "

"You know, Jean, I admire your loyalty to your friends, but I'm rather afraid I just can't be of much help. There is a tissue sample on file, but that can be examined only with the consent of the family. Somehow I don't feature that taking place. The rest of your suspicions are, if you excuse the expression, little more that womanly intuition. The telephone threat is real, but that should be handled through your local police. They could put a tap on your phone to record any threatening calls and identify the origins if any should occur again," Fred offered as a consolation.

"So, there's no way that we could "borrow" the tissue sample?" John queried.

"You know very well from your experience as a homicide investigator, John, that any evidence used against a suspect must be impeccable. Purloined, illegal evidence is a big NO NO," Fred countered.

"I tell you what I will do for you. Since this was initially a homicide investigation, I'll speak to the chief and see what he thinks would be the possibility of reopening it. I still think that there is slim to no hope that it will happen. However, stranger thinks have taken place in the realms of police work."

With little more to discuss and realizing that this was the end of a long shift for Fred, Jean and John thanked him for his help and asked him to please keep them informed.

The trip across town to the Doubletree was filled with glum silence. Finally Jean sighed, "I don't really know what I expected. Just that somewhere, somehow, someone would listen and be able to figure this out."

"Hey, Jean, don't be gloomy. We have planted the seeds for a possible reopening. May just be that this cold case will come out of hiding when we least expect it."

After a quick good night, Jean unlocked her door and flipped on the TV. Somehow the trivia of a *Friends* repeat did little to console her. She surfed the channels in a lackluster manner and almost in a fit of pique snapped the off button on the TV and turned out the light. After plumping the pillows for the fourth time, ripping the blanket from the foot of the bed, and breathing slowly and consistently for five minutes, she heard a gentle knock at the door.

After checking the peep hole, Jean unlocked the door to see a familiar face and a gentle, comforting voice, "Hey, Jean Queen, let's give it a rest for the night."

Chapter 22
Keep the Lady Happy

After a scrambled egg breakfast in the in the motel's coffee shop, Jean and John had a smooth trip back to Spokane. Amusedly, Jean wondered if John's improved mood this morning could be explained by the copious cups of coffee they had as they lingered over at breakfast, or if it might just have been something else. At any rate, she found herself humming snitches of a song from Oklahoma— "Your eyes mustn't glow like mine…" as the miles sailed by.

Fall foliage was just beginning to turn, the river was a brilliant blue, and somehow the problems of tissue samples, homicide investigations, and autopsy reports faded into the background as Jean chatted with John about her years spent in the classroom.

"So much of teaching revolves around calendars and schedules and bells. In some ways it was good to let go of that," she confided as she gazed contentedly out the window. "Nevertheless, the fall always makes me a bit nostalgic for the excitement of a new school year. The honeymoon usually lasted until about the end of October. The kids were still enthused about class activities and often responded rather excitedly, even to zany assignments. My favorite was reading Jonathan Livingston Seagull, a rather inspirational allegory about a lowly gull that achieved great heights. Do you ever remember reading it, John?'

"Actually, literature was not one of my favorite subjects," he confessed somewhat contritely. "The honeymoon with my teacher didn't ever really take hold…when I was young, that is," John grinned happily.

Hoping against hope that the sun reflecting from the dash was covering her blushing cheeks, Jean continued, "Well, anyway, one of the 'be all that you can be' activities I used to love involved having the kids find music to reflect that very theme. They had to record a snippet of the song, play it for the class, and explain the connection."

"Jeeze, I wish you had been my teacher. That assignment would have been a breeze. Criminey, all I remember about English classes is diagramming those darn sentences. Conquering the direction of the lines was almost more than I could handle."

"Approaches to teaching have indeed changed over the years," Jean confessed. "And speaking of your response to that assignment, you know the 'I Can Fly' song? I did get that a number of times, and I still smile when I remember once when it came time for one of my students to explain the connection."

"That part seems almost self explanatory," puzzled John.

"True, but this particular young man won my heart when he explained that not only was there a connection between Jonathan and the character in the song, but that he had chosen it because he knew Miss Smiley would love it."

"Now that was one smart lad," John countered. "And I'll bet he is one successful young man. Keeping a lady happy should be at the front and center of any gentleman's agenda."

The miles flew by, traffic was relatively light, and it seemed only minutes after crossing the Idaho state line that they were sailing over the Washington border, approaching the Sullivan exit, and cruising down Mission Street toward their turnoff and respective homes. The last few miles had been spent in companionable silence without a hint of awkwardness. "Well, really," Jean chided herself, "we have passed the awkward stage."

Her reflection was interrupted by John muttering under his breath, something about "abandoned cars cluttering up the neighborhood."

"What are you muttering about, John?" she asked absently.

"Think I'd better get on the phone and report that rusty heap of a green car parked in front of Bremer's house. I think it's about a 1952 Pontiac. See if you can snag the license number as we drive by."

As they slowly approached the car, which was indeed an old Pontiac Bonneville, it roared to life and zoomed down the road in front of them.

"So much for an abandoned car, John. And by the way, I didn't really get a look at the license plate. Didn't look like a Washington one, though. Maybe Montana, but I'm not sure"

"One less thing to take care of this afternoon. Let me help you get your things inside, and we'll give some thought to dinner."

A purring Mrs. Robinson greeted them at the front door as John placed Jean's duffle bag in the front entry. "I'll give you a call in a bit," he promised glancing at the telephone on the hall table. "By the way, your message light is on alert."

"Mmm, wonder who that could be? Let me check quickly."

"Soooo, lady, you don't know the meaning of BUTT OUT? You must have a dictionary, or MAYBE I can be a little more clear. KEEP YOUR NOSE OUT OF MATTERS THAT DO NOT CONCERN YOU." A sharp click ended the one-sided conversation, and Jean scowled unhappily at the "Welcome Home Intrusion."

"So much for home, sweet home," Jean gulped. "What do we do now, John?"

"I don't like this one bit," he growled. "Is there some way to check the time that call came in?"

"Yes, the time recorded is Sunday, 4:02 am."

"Well, one thing I do know for sure. I do not want you to stay here alone at night." John growled.

Jean's reaction vacillated between being comforted and bristling at any attempt to threaten her independence. Ironically, she assumed the position of "the calm one," and she tried to reassure John that a threatening phone call was indeed disturbing, but didn't really pose much physical danger. "Tell you what Mr. Protective Policeman, why don't I square things away here and run down to Rosauer's for some steaks. We can grill them in the back yard, and I'll bake some potatoes and whip up a salad. Planning our strategy will surely be easier if we have something good to eat."

"I really don't think that some things require any planning, but you know what your students always did."

"What on earth are you talking about now, John?"

"Keep the lady happy, My Dear. Keep the lady happy."

Chapter 23
The Tide Is Turning

Jean hurriedly made her way to the meat department where she selected two great looking T-bone steaks. Romaine, mushrooms, and tomatoes for a salad, and a loaf of French bread completed her mission, and she checked out in record time.

Still pondering the mysterious phone call, she meandered her way through the parking lot toward her car. Suddenly she heard a car accelerate behind her. She had only a moment to throw herself and her cart between two parked cars

"Breathe, breathe," was all Jean could say to herself as she lay in a crumpled heap on the cement in the parking lot. The trembling did not subside, so she decided to try to roll over. It was not as easy as she thought it would be. "Oh, Lord, I will be so sore and black and blue tomorrow. I can hardly move already!" she whispered to herself. Finally able to roll over, she tried to sit up. Though creaky and groaning all the way, she was able to do so. She shook her head as if to get rid of the cobwebs and looked around. She could hear the screeching of gears as the car that had tried to hit her accelerated out of the parking lot.

Looking back toward Rosauers, she saw an older couple rushing toward her. "Are you okay?" the man asked in a very concerned voice. "We saw what happened. What was wrong with that young fella, anyway?"

The white-haired woman with him knelt down and patted Jean's arm. "Do you think we should call an ambulance?" she inquired.

"No, I think I am fine, just going to be very sore and multicolored for several days," Jean replied.

"Can you get up?" the man asked.

"I think so…if you give me a hand or two," Jean said.

The kindly man and woman positioned themselves on both sides of Jean and helped her to her feet. They were hesitant to let go of her as she was still trembling. "Why don't you let me call someone for you? I have my cell phone right here," the gentleman said as he flourished his phone in the palm of his right hand.

"No, thank you very much, but I am sure I will be all right. My car is just down this lane two more slots. I have a cold Diet Coke in one of my sacks. When I get inside the car, I'll just rest there, drink my Coke, and then go home. It's not far to go," Jean replied, smiling at the couple.

"Well, we saw what happened. I think you should report this to the police. What do you think, Marie?" the man stated, looking at his companion.

"I don't know if it was an accident or on purpose, but if you ask me, it looked like he tried to hit you. Maybe he was just playing chicken, but I think I would certainly call the police," Marie replied seriously.

"Well, I am okay, and I do not think it was on purpose," Jean lied. She smiled at the couple and looked at the woman, "I think you may be right. It probably was just some fool kid playing chicken. Did you get a good look at the driver?"

"No," Marie said, "we were just too far away to see anything clearly. The only thing I really noticed was he looked like he was around 20 or so and was wearing a white baseball cap. That and the horrible, old, green car. It looked like it needed an extreme makeover!"

The elderly gentleman thrust out his hand and said, "I'm John Boswell, and this is my dear friend Marie Griffin. I will give you my

YVONNE DEITZ, VIKKI MOORMANN, SUSAN SCHREIBER

card if you decide later you need to call the police. We will be glad to tell what we saw. I only wish we could tell you more." He dug through his pocket and took out a small business card case. He withdrew one card and handed it to Jean. As he put the case back in his pocket, he continued, "I think we had better walk you to your car after we gather up your runaway cart. I want to make sure you are completely okay before you drive anywhere."

They walked Jean to her car, gathered up her grocery cart, put the grocery sacks in the back seat, and then once Jean was seated, asked again, "Are you sure you are okay? We can sit here with you for a while if you would like us to."

Jean could not believe her luck to have encountered two such nice people. "Thanks, I am quite okay now. I don't even think I need to sit here longer and drink a Coke. I am feeling quite in control of myself and would like to just go home and take a long, hot, soothing bath."

The couple nodded goodbye, smiled, and walked back toward their car. Jean pondered, "My goodness, I guess my guardian angel was watching over me today. Not only did she protect me from that car but also provided me with two lovely people to help me out." As she tried to brush off the rest of the dirt from her blouse and slacks, she murmured, "Thank you, Lord, for keeping me safe!" Jean started to brush off the knees of her pants when she noticed her new slacks had been torn. She examined the tear and felt chagrined. The tear was on the bias and probably never could be repaired without looking exactly like what it would be, a mend job. "Why me?" she thought disgustedly. "Why my new slacks?"

Jean shook her head, turned on the ignition, and drove carefully out of the parking lot. As she traveled the short distance back to her home, she began to feel angry. The closer she got to her home, the angrier she became, and the more she thought about what had just happened. When she pulled into her driveway, she was just boiling. She was so angry, she had not even noticed John just ten feet away from her driveway, tending to his rose bushes while he awaited her return from the supermarket. Jean tried to climb out of the car; however, the body was certainly not cooperating. "Oowwwwwww," she moaned as she finally was able to ease her battered body from the sedan.

Upon hearing her moaning, John turned to see what was going on. He was appalled at what he saw and rushed to Jean's side exclaiming, "What the hell happened to you?"

Jean smiled at John feebly and replied, "Well, I went to Rosauers to get our groceries. I was returning to my car with my cart when an old, battered green car tried to play catch me if you can. He didn't win, but it was a close contest. I ended up splayed on the cement between two parked cars."

"You poor baby," John murmured as he took her purse and keys in one hand and guided her toward her house.

After he got her inside and settled on the couch with Mrs. Robinson cuddling against her comfortingly, he said, "Okay, I'll get you a couple of aspirin and a glass of water. Do you want me to put on the kettle for some tea?"

Jean smiled and replied, "Yes, the aspirin and water would be great; however, I just want to get in a hot tub. Could I ask you, please, to bring in the groceries?"

"Sure enough," John replied as he handed her the aspirin and water. "Let me go start a bath for you," and he was off to start the hot water running in the tub.

Mrs. Robinson watched Jean for a moment and then came over to rub against her legs as if to offer solace.

When he returned to the living room, he said, "The water is just about ready. I put some Epsom salts in and also some bubble bath I found on the shelf when I looked for the salts."

Jean grimaced and tried to get up, and John gently lifted her. He guided her toward the bathroom and then asked," Are you going to be able to get in the tub okay? I can stay and help you if necessary."

"I'll tell you what I am going to do. I'll get undressed and see how I am doing, then try to get into the tub. If I can't do it by myself, I'll let you know, okay?" Jean replied determinedly.

"Okay, but you know I am here for you if you need me!" John commented. "I am simply going to sit in the hall until you come out. That way I'll know if you need anything. I'll bring in the groceries in a bit."

Jean heard John position a chair just outside the bathroom door with Mrs. Robinson offering her take on the situation and smiled to herself. "I am so glad they are an important part of my life," she murmured to herself as she shed her clothing.

As John heard various sounds ranging from "Ooooohs" and "Ahhhs" issuing from the bathroom with Mrs. Robinson emitting soft meows each time, he checked to make sure Jean was still doing okay. When he finally went out to the car to get Jean's groceries, he raged to himself, "When Jean is feeling better, I will find out what the hell went on!"

When Jean finally emerged from the bathroom, she was looking better. The scrapes on her forearms and hands were red, but the blood had been washed away, and John could tell antiseptic cream had been applied liberally. When she sat down on the couch once again, her robe parted slightly, and John saw the ugly scrapes on her knees. He tried to maintain his cool but discovered it wasn't easy.

"Okay, he said with forced calmness, "now tell me exactly what happened."

"There's not much to tell," Jean replied. "I was walking back to my car with my grocery cart. I was almost there when I heard a car coming fast behind me. I just had time to look behind me, see the fast-approaching car, push my cart between two parked cars, and dive after it. I must not have done that too gracefully because I ended up sprawled on the cement between the two parked cars as the oncoming car whooshed by me."

John questioned, "Did you get a look at the driver?"

Jean answered, "No, I really didn't, but the older couple who saw it happen said they thought he was about 20 or so."

"What old couple?" John inquired.

"Oh, John Boswell and Marie Griffin. They were walking to their car when they saw it happen." She slowly reached down for her purse, retrieved it with a minimum of groans and handed Boswell's card to John. "Here's his card," Jean replied and handed it to her friend. "They were so sweet and worried about me. I need to send them a note of thanks to let them know everything is fine. I really appreciate all their help and concern."

"What can you tell me about the car?" John continued.

"Not much, I am afraid. It was green, old, and battered," Jean said calmly. "You know, it kind of reminded me of that old, green car parked out front when we came home from Missoula."

"Were you able to get the license plate number?" John asked.

"No, it happened too quickly," Jean answered.

"Well, maybe the police will find the vehicle," John commented and then saw the look on Jean's face. "You did call the police, didn't you?"

"No, not exactly. I thought I could just tell you," Jean said, looking down at her fingertips.

John stood up and stated, "I am going to call the police now. They will send someone to talk to you when they can. I am also going to my house to call Fred to tell him what happened. We just cannot ignore this, Jean! Where is his number?"

"I know," Jean murmured still looking at her hands, "but why not call Fred from here? I feel better just having you with me."

John's face softened and said, "Of course, I'll stay with you. Where do you keep your phone book and address book?"

"In the bottom drawer of my desk just inside the dining room," Jean replied.

John went over, retrieved the phone book, called the local police, and then turned to Jean to tell her, "An officer will be here in about forty-five minutes. Now for Fred." John was lucky and was able to get a hold of Fred directly. While John talked with Fred, Jean tried to flip through a magazine she had been meaning to read. She was surprised to hear John punch numbers on the phone again after he ended the conversation with Fred.

When John returned to the couch, he sat down gingerly, trying not to jar her. He smiled and said, "Fred agrees with me. You need to file a police report."

Jean just nodded her agreement.

John continued, "He also told me that he was able to talk to his boss about reopening Bill's case. It seems Hugo Manheim, the once temporary coroner, is in trouble about two other cases where he did sloppy work, so Fred's boss said since they were reopening the other

131

two cases, they might as well do Bill's, too. They have ordered a toxicology screen on the tissue sample. Since Dr. South, the regular coroner, is back, he will be doing the test. Fred has complete faith in the good doctor. The results will be available in about a week."

"Additionally," John said, "I called an old contact at the phone company and asked if she could tell me the number your harassing phone calls were made from and possibly an address. She promised to look up that information."

Jean leaned her battered, bruised body against John and half whispered, "I wonder if they will find anything, and if they do, what will it be?"

Chapter 24
What About the Test?

Jean began to feel a little more relaxed after a relatively uneventful week, although there were times when she was aware of the muscles in her neck and shoulders tightening as if she were waiting for the other shoe to fall. Still, there had been no more threatening phone calls and no more sightings of the green Pontiac.

She allowed herself to linger over a second cup of coffee and the morning paper when her phone rang at 8:30 on Tuesday morning. She smiled when she recognized Mary Carol's voice on the other end of the line.

"Hey! It's good to hear your voice," Jean told her warmly. "What's up over there? Are you off work today, or did you decide to join the ranks of us retired folks all of a sudden?"

Mary Carol laughed. "Mostly I still slave away at the office, but my boss is having some painting done in the reception room, so he decided to close down for a few days. He took off to play some golf and gave me a couple of days of free time, too, which is nice.

"I thought you might be interested to hear some news that Crystal shared with me last night. She was pretty upset, and I have to admit that it bothered me a bit, too, so I thought I'd just run this by you and try to get a level-headed handle on all of it."

Jean felt her stomach tighten as she asked, "What kind of news did Crystal have?"

"Well, she told me that when Bill's body was found in the river, there was a police investigation of his death, which we knew was a matter of routine procedure. Crystal also said they had concluded that Bill's death was an accidental drowning, which we all knew was true. The thing that has Crystal so upset is the fact that the authorities have reopened the investigation. We all know how emotional Crystal is, and when she was telling me about this, she practically became hysterical, and it took about two hours of listening, patting her shoulder, cajoling her, and plying her with wine to get her to calm down before she went home.

"I didn't sleep too well myself last night, I have to admit. I told Fred about it, but he said he really wasn't free to discuss it with me at this stage, so I wanted to call you and just get it off my chest. The whole thing gives me the creeps, and I really feel sorry for Crystal. She's been through so much, and she kept crying and saying things about how they need to let Bill rest in peace and let her have some peace, too, and allow her to get on with her life."

Jean took a deep breath and another sip of her coffee before allowing herself to respond to any of this news. She must have miscalculated her breathing and sipping timing because before she could say a word, she choked and coughed.

"Jean, are you all right?" Mary Carol asked with genuine concern.

Jean coughed a response and then answered between gasps, "I'm fine...just fine. Cough! Cough!" In a strangled voice she managed to say, "Or I will be just as soon as I can breathe!"

"What happened? Did you swallow down the wrong pipe or something?"

Jean cleared her throat. "That's exactly what I did. I was sipping coffee when you called, and I guess I tried to swallow and talk at the wrong time for a minute. I'm sorry."

"No problem," answered Mary Carol. I'm just glad you're okay. One friend at a time is enough to worry about."

"I agree with you about that, for sure. I'm sorry to hear about Crystal and this…this new problem she's facing."

Jean thought this might be a good time to change the subject. "Speaking of friends, have you happened to see Max lately?"

"Not so much Max as his car," Mary Carol said rather slowly. It seems to be parked outside Crystal's house quite frequently, in fact, nearly every day when she is in the area and not traveling about promoting the work of one of her latest artists."

Jean cleared her throat again and asked, "Has Crystal said anything to you about Max or about his frequent visits to her place?"

"Yes, after I said something about noticing his car and asked how he was doing, she told me she was getting a little uncomfortable about Max appearing on her doorstep so frequently, and she hoped the neighbors wouldn't think anything about it. She said she felt sorry for him after his split with Beth, and she was grateful for all his help in getting things together after Bill died, so she didn't want to discourage his coming over so much. She thinks he is probably just lonely and needs someone to talk to. But she also said she was a little relieved that she would be going with her latest protégé on his European tour to promote his work. She thinks it will be good to get away for a little while."

"Hmmm," said Jean thoughtfully. "No doubt. That will probably help distract her from this latest development regarding Bill's death, too. Crystal always has been a very emotional individual, but she seems to be pretty strong, too. She has done amazingly well in adjusting to the loss of Bill, I think. If you talk to her at all about art or about her foundation to help promote young artists, she seems to become a different person, full of energy and even enthusiastic. I really don't think you need to worry too much about Crystal, Mary Carol. I think Crystal can take care of herself pretty well in the long run."

"Oh, Jean, I knew I'd feel better after I talked to you, and I do. You always seem to have a good, sensible view of things, and you always know the right thing to say to make me feel better." Mary Carol sighed a little. "Thanks so much, Sweetie!"

YVONNE DEITZ, VIKKI MOORMANN, SUSAN SCHREIBER

"You're more than welcome, M.C. I don't know that I always have the right take on things, but I'm glad I was able to help you out a bit this time."

"So am I, and how is everything going over in your neck of the woods since we last talked?"

The events of the past weeks flew through Jean's mind, but she dismissed them quickly and said, "Just fine. Mrs. Robinson is as bossy as ever." Then she smiled to herself and added, "I've been busy with yard work and thinking about getting things buttoned down for the coming winter. My neighbor, John Houck, has been advising me on some of those things, and that's been a big help to me, and I appreciate it a lot." In her mind she added, "And that isn't all I appreciate about John!"

"Well, I'm glad all is well with you, Jean. You take care of Mrs. R. and yourself, and thanks again for listening."

"No problem. You take care of yourself, too, and give my best to your special friend Fred."

Thinking about Mary Carol and Fred made Jean smile and feel warm inside, but a small chill entered in and tightened her shoulders when she thought about the investigation into Bill's death opening up again. This was, after all, what she had wanted. Or was it? Jean's stomach knotted slightly as she thought about what the investigation might reveal.

Throughout the day Jean had watched for any sign of John's presence next door, but she had seen none. She knew he had planned to spend the day doing various errands: getting his hair cut, paying bills, checking on some tools at the hardware store, and doing various kinds of shopping for groceries and whatever, but she really felt she needed to tell him about Mary Carol's news. She wanted to talk to him now, but she chided herself, "Whoa! You've got to give the man some space. You can't expect him to be available to you every hour of the day."

Jean busied herself with her own household chores, and by the end of the day her carpets were clean, the furniture was dusted, and both bathrooms had the fresh scent of lemon cleaner and disinfectant. All this gave her a feeling of satisfaction as she washed her supper dishes when the phone rang.

"Maybe that's John," she thought as she dried her hands on a towel and picked up the kitchen phone. The masculine voice on the other end was not John's, however, but Fred's in Missoula.

"Hi, Jean. Fred Williamson here." He got right to the point. "I thought you would want to hear the results of the tests they did on the tissue sample of Bill Pemberton. Some of your concerns are apparently well founded. There was evidence of DMSO in Pemberton's system along with an extremely large dose of tranquilizers. However, our police report showed no tranquilizers of any kind found anywhere in Pemberton's things. I placed a call to his doctor, Robert Sheffield, and asked about prescriptions Pemberton had been given, and there was nothing that even remotely resembled a tranquilizer of any kind. It appears that your friend's death could very likely have been the result of foul play."

After being cautioned by Fred to be very careful about sharing this information and thanking him for his call, Jean hung up the phone just long enough to insure getting a dial tone and dialed John's number.

Chapter 25
Please Join Us

A week had passed, and as Jean walked slowly down the drive to the mailbox, she pondered the threat of rain. "It might as well," she muttered grumpily to herself. "Nothing else seems to be going right." Scooping up the contents of the box, she leafed through the Safeway ad, a bill from Avista, and two rather interesting envelopes in lovely, ivory vellum. "What on earth could this be?" she wondered out loud. "I can't recall that any of my former students have wedding plans.

Please join us
For a preview
of Greg Applebee's
European tour
Friday, Sept. 30, and
Saturday, October 1, 2000

Mezzanine of the
Davenport Hotel

Sponsored by
Northwest Art
Foundation

"My, my," Jean thought warily, "Crystal strikes again. She promised me an invitation, and it seems she is true to her word. I wonder how Max feels about her trundling off to Europe. Should be interesting to meet this Applebee person. I wonder what kind of a turnout they will have in good old Spokane."

She heard the beginning of a soft pattering of rain on the roof as she opened the second envelope. This too was rather craftily done, but not quite as formal as the first.

PLEASE COME!

Why? A bon voyage party for Crystal Pemberton and Greg Applebee

Where? Aboard the Mishanock at the Independence Point Dock—Coeur d'Alene, Idaho

When? 1 o'clock, Sunday, October 2

Cocktails and hors d' oeuvres

RSVP: Willy Pemberton
(509) 466-8790

"Indeed, it looks like a full social calendar for next weekend." Jean thought. I hope I can persuade John to go. There should be several Missoula people there, and it might just be a good chance to tie up some loose ends. I hope the weather clears up. I do look forward to a golden October, and a wet weather boat trip doesn't sound too inviting."

She heard a funny noise behind her. She turned to see Mrs. Robinson shredding the envelopes she had swiped from the swing seat. "Oh, you little imp! You really don't like Crystal, do you?"

At that her spirits lifted in spite of the rain, which was now coming down at a very good clip. The events of the past few weeks seemed to dissipate with the falling raindrops. She even thought briefly of breaking into song, "Rain drops keep falling on my head, but that doesn't mean my eyes will soon be turning red...," but thought better of if when she realized she couldn't quite grasp the tune.

Not quite sure what to do with the rest of the afternoon, Jean wandered down the front steps and cut through the hedge to see if John were home. After all, she did have to get the weekend squared away, and perhaps he had heard something from the police. Most of her scrapes and bruises were fading, but she still had moments of stiffness when she moved very quickly. Neither did she really sleep very soundly or peacefully with the possibility of a shrill telephone call always in the back of her mind.

Just as she raised her hand for a gentle rap at the door, it opened as if by magic. "And what, little girl, are you selling? You may certainly sign me up for at least a dozen boxes. Girl Scout Cookies, you say? My favorite is the peanut butter ones, but the mint variety is delicious, too. Please come in and let me taste your wares."

"You nut! I do hope you know better than to entice a poor little Girl Scout inside your door."

"You forget, madam; I was a highly trained officer of the law. You're not selling cookies, you say? Then it must be sugar you have come for. A cup? Two? You must be baking cookies. How could I have been so confused?"

"John, if you don't cut it with the cookie chatter, I am going to march right back out the door."

"Okay, okay! Come on in, and we'll have a cup of tea. If only we had some cookies...sorry. I really promise this time."

"I came to see if you would be interested in going with me this weekend to an art show at the Davenport Hotel on Saturday and then a bon voyage party in Coeur d'Alene on Sunday. All in honor of— none other than our friend Crystal Pemberton, the prima donna of Montana Art."

"Sounds like a plan to me," John responded. "Speaking of Missoula, I had an interesting conversation with Fred Williamson this morning. Sit down while I brew up this tea for you and I'll tell you all about it."

"Yes, Captain. Anything you say."

"Fred tells me that he has done some investigation into the properties of DMSO. We probably know it best as a horse liniment, but it is often used as a treatment for arthritis on humans. It has the ability to penetrate the skin very quickly and to act as a vehicle for soothing muscles. Now if it were accompanied by a tranquilizer, that, too, would be put into the blood stream and create confusion or even downright drowsiness. Let's imagine the worst case scenario and couple it with the confusion of Alzheimer's and a rushing stream. Standing upright might prove to be a BIG problem. If there had been a formal autopsy complete with a toxicology screening performed initially, this might have come to light. Sloppy police work saved the day for somebody. Remember I told you a long time ago that the facts usually win out. In this case, it just took a bit longer for them to surface. No pun intended. "

"Gracious. The plot thickens. Seems like we have several facts at hand, and now we need to connect the dots to motive and murderer. It still boggles my mind to cast Crystal and Max in the heinous roll of husband killer. And what of the phone calls and the green car incident? Maybe we are getting just a little too close."

"I heard from my contact at the phone company. She gave me the number and address from which your harassing phone calls came. I checked it out, but it was only a public phone on the corner of Pines and Sprague. No leads there, unfortunately, but stick with me, Babe, and we will connect those dots. Maybe we should take our paint brushes to the art show and see what we come up with."

"I declare, John, you should have been a star English student. You are worth a metaphor a minute."

"Met-a-four. Isn't that the one about Will Rogers? He never met a four that he didn't like? Oh, no. I know. It's like the Met who got on base on four."

"STOP. STOP. You have just sacrificed your position as the head of the class. I am terribly afraid that you have sealed your position as class clown," Jean hooted.

"But Miss Smiley, ma'am, it surely seems like you are looking like your name. And I do believe the rain has let up."

Chapter 26
How Much Does the Art Show Show?

"I've found out a couple more interesting facts about DMSO," John stated seriously as he and Jean were driving into Spokane toward the Davenport Hotel and the showing of Greg Applebee's art.

"Oh, really, and what might they be?" Jean asked and turned to look at the unusually solemn face next to her.

"Well, for one thing, whoever was responsible for mixing the heavy-duty tranquilizer with the DMSO obviously did some research and planning beforehand. Normally the DMSO has a powerful odor associated with it, and most people would not want to use it for that reason unless they were experiencing very severe pain. There is an odorless DMSO that has been developed, but it's fairly recent, and not everyone is aware of that type yet. Do you know if Bill was having problems with arthritis where the pain was strong enough that he might be willing to try some of the more common, stinky kind of DMSO?"

"I really don't know anything about that," Jean replied thoughtfully, "but I could ask Robert Sheffield about it if I can think of some logical reason to be asking," and she took a small notebook from her purse and made a few notes in it. Beth about it," and she took a small notebook from her purse and made a few notes in it.

Noticing what she was doing, John reached over and patted her knee with a smile. "Ever the Miss Efficient School Teacher, aren't you?"

"You'd better believe it!" Jean smiled back.

At that moment John pulled the car into the parking garage of the Davenport, handed his keys over to a valet for parking, and walked around to the passenger side where Jean was emerging from the car with the help of another valet.

"My arm, Ms. Smiley," John bowed slightly as he extended his left arm to Jean and smiled at her.

"Thank you, Sir," she smiled back and took his arm.

"I can hardly wait to feast my eyes on this gorgeous lady that you have described to me," John teased as they walked into the hotel lobby. "I wonder if she will be in need of an escort to take her home after the show. You wouldn't mind hailing a cab would you if that's the case?"

"Of course not if you will supply me with the cab fare all the way back to the Spokane Valley. I don't really think you will need to drive Crystal home after the show, though. I think she is staying right here in the hotel for both days and probably Sunday, too, because of the farewell cruise in Coeur d'Alene. Maybe you would like to drive her home to Missoula after that, though. Do you want me to pick up your mail for you while you are gone? Water your lawn? Anything else?"

"Ah, Ms. Smiley, I was hoping to stir up a tiny bit of jealousy in that cold heart of yours. Instead, you are just too cool. I'm really crushed, you know." John gave her shoulders a quick hug, kissed her cheek, and they crossed the magnificent lobby of the hotel and started up the wide, carpeted stairs to the mezzanine. "If I haven't mentioned it already, you do look quite nice in that blue dress you are wearing tonight," he said with an appreciative glance at Jean's aqua silk suit.

"Thank you, and you look rather handsome yourself." Jean smiled back with sparkling eyes. "It's amazing what a nicely cut suit and a haircut can do for a man," she teased.

As they entered the mezzanine area, they were greeted by the sound of a string quartet in the background and a long table with tall champagne flutes, cocktail plates and napkins and a wide variety of tempting appetizers in the foreground. About a dozen people were sipping champagne, nibbling on appetizers, and looking at the canvases positioned on easels all around the area.

While a wine steward was filling glasses for Jean and John, Crystal spotted them and sauntered over holding the hand of a tall, handsome, blond, young man. Crystal looked magnificent, as usual, wearing a pencil-slim, burgundy, satin dress. The spaghetti straps showed off her creamy, ivory skin, and her thick, dark hair was piled on top of her head. Sparkling diamonds dangled from her ears and were the only jewelry she wore.

"Jean, dear, I'm so glad you came! I want you to meet the reason for this wonderful showing, Greg Applebee. Greg, this is a long-time friend of mine, Jean Smiley. And you," she said turning to John, "must be a friend of Jean's. I'm so glad you came with her."

Crystal dropped Greg's hand and held hers out to John, who took it and told her, "I'm glad I came with Jean, too. I'm John Houck, and you must be Crystal."

"Yes, I am. Greg, why don't you show Miss Smiley the pieces we have on display here, and I'll show John around."

Before Greg could say anything, John took Jean's hand and said, "You really don't have to show us anything. We actually prefer to walk around and look at pictures at our own speed so we can talk about what we are seeing with each other, don't we, Honey?"

"Yes, we do." Jean gave John a relieved smile and then turned to Greg. "Really nice meeting you, Greg. Crystal, thanks for this opportunity to see what this young man has done. I'm eager to see his work, and we'll probably have a chance to visit a little at the party in Coeur d'Alene on Sunday.

"Oh, is that Max I see over there in the corner? John, I'd like to introduce you to Max, too. He was another classmate of ours. Thanks again, Crystal, and we'll plan to see you on Sunday."

Crystal looked momentarily flustered; Greg didn't quite know what to do, and Jean and John headed toward the corner of the room where Max appeared to be looking intently at a painting.

Greg's paintings were realistic, quite detailed, and included scenes depicting mountains and lakes familiar to western Montana, northern Idaho, and parts of Washington. Some pictures showed hunters, trappers, and Indians from days gone by. All showed a land that was pristine and unencumbered with any modern developments to speak of. Those who were viewing the paintings murmured words of praise for the young man's efforts. Jean and John found themselves pleasantly surprised at the quality of the realism, and so they were surprised to find Max glowering at the painting before him.

"Hello, Max," Jean began. "It's nice to see you here. I want you to meet a good friend and neighbor of mine."

Max looked up rather startled out of his apparently dark thoughts, and attempted a weak smile in answer to Jean's greeting. "Jean! Nice to see you. A good friend and neighbor? Guess that would be you, eh?" he said turning to John and extending his hand.

"Right. John Houck," John replied as he shook Max's hand. And you're Max...Max..."

"Milner," Max stated. "Glad to meet you, John."

"Likewise, Max. That's an interesting picture you're studying there. The boy seems to like realism in an idealistic kind of way."

"Romantic art," Jean added.

"What makes you say that?" demanded Max, his voice rising slightly. The painting he had been staring at showed a young Indian maiden bathing in a small stream in a sequestered area with tall mountains in the background. Her clothing lay on the ground nearby, and her dark hair flowed around her face and shoulders. Her face was lifted toward the sky, and it looked slightly familiar.

"Romantic simply refers to the fact that it is ideal," Jean stated matter-of-factly. "You don't see any thorns on the bushes or ugly weeds growing anywhere. Everything is perfect including the features of the Indian maid, and I think every woman wishes she had a body like that."

"Oh," was all Max could say. Then he added, "I wonder who his model was for this picture."

"Well, I wouldn't know, of course, but there's something about the face that reminds me of his patron Crystal Pemberton," John said cautiously as he studied the picture and stroked his chin.

"You think so?" Max questioned, and then added, "Oh, excuse me. There is something I needed to talk to her about a minute before I have to leave," and he hurried off without another word.

Jean looked at John with raised eyebrows, and John simply took her hand and led her to the next painting. They continued looking and edging their way over to where Max and Crystal were standing and talking in rather hushed tones. When they were closer to the couple, both of them heard Max blurt out in a stage whisper, "Crystal, you know that I would do anything...anything for you, and I have proved that!" They kept their backs turned as they heard Max leave.

Chapter 27
Misadventure on the Mishanock

"I just don't understand why Mary Carol didn't want to stay with me," Jean lamented as John pulled off the freeway onto the first Coeur d'Alene exit. "Why do she and Fred have to waste the money to stay in a motel here in Coeur d'Alene?"

John smiled and replied, "Well, maybe they wanted to be alone and have some quiet time."

"I wouldn't have bothered them, and with Fred staying next door with you, it would have been convenient for both of them," Jean retorted.

"I think," John commented while he reached over to hold her hand in his, "that perhaps they just want to be together. You know, TOGETHER."

"Well, they could have been together at my house...oh, you mean TOGETHER. Now I get it. Oh, what a dummy I am," Jean mumbled.

John smiled, gave her hand a reassuring squeeze, and kept alert as the traffic on Northwest Boulevard was heavy on this beautiful Sunday afternoon.

As they neared Independence Point, John asked, "Where do you think I should park?"

"Let's try the parking lot right by the lake at Independence Point first since it is so close to the boat. If that's full, I guess we will have to drive around looking for a spot," Jean answered.

As they pulled into the lot, they saw Mary Carol and Fred getting out of Fred's pickup. John honked and waved as Jean exclaimed, "There's one. That car is just pulling out." John maneuvered his SUV around into the first lane and waited patiently for the older car to abandon his previous spot. Then John slid his car into the spot smoothly, and John and Jean gathered together the things they wanted to take with them.

As Jean got out of the car, she heard Mary Carol calling her name. She turned just in time to be engulfed in a bear hug by Fred. Laughing, she exclaimed, "Gee, I like how you greet old friends!"

The four walked down toward the dock and the Mishanock, one of the lake's cruise ships, in the exceptionally warm autumn sun. Mary Carol stretched her arms toward the sun and said," I cannot believe it is October already. It feels like late August. I wonder how long this weather will last?"

Just as Jean started to answer Mary Carol, she realized that the couple right ahead of them was Willy, Crystal's son, and his wife, Margie, so she called out to them instead, "Willy, how are you? And, Margie, that is a darling shorts set. You two look ready for a relaxing afternoon in the sun."

Willy laughed and responded as he held up a big tote bag, "We certainly are. Well, at least one of us is. I think Margie has plans to soak up some last minute rays while I zoom around making sure everything is okay."

Mary Carol added, "It certainly was great of you to put on this shindig for your mom and Greg. I am just really glad we were able to make it. Fred had to work last night, so we drove over this morning."

Willy replied looking at all four of them, "I am glad you all could make it. There will be plenty of people from the foundation to give my mom and Greg support professionally, but there is nothing like old friends to make the day special. Even Max will be here! There

will be an open bar if you don't like champagne, and the hors
d'oeuvres should feed a small army. I even hired a trio to be playing
in the main salon." As they boarded the boat, Willy added, "Well,
have a good time. I have a million things to do." He turned toward
Margie, held out the large tote, and said, "Here, Honey, is all your
tanning paraphernalia. I couldn't find your tanning lotion, so I threw
in an old bottle I had in the bathroom. Your pillow, towel, and
magazines are also in there, so you should have a good time. It's a
perfect day on the lake." He gave Margie a big hug, waved to the
foursome, and then dashed into the salon to help greet the guests.

Margie laughed and said, "Isn't that just like Willy, always taking
care of others? He is so much like his dad was. Well, I am off to the
upper deck to get some rays. Have fun and come up and join me if
you get bored." She turned toward the stairs to the upper deck.

"Let's go do the politically correct 'meet and greet' first; then we
can have some fun together," Jean commented as she looked toward
Mary Carol, Fred, and John. They nodded their agreement, and in
unison the foursome moved toward the main salon.

There was a big sign at the door proclaiming Greg Applebee as
the Northwest Art Foundation's newest star. Right behind the sign
were Crystal, Greg, and Willy greeting everyone as they came on
board and into the salon. There were about thirty people already in
the room, and as Jean turned around, she was surprised to see even
more people coming.

When they approached Crystal, she warmly welcomed them each
by name. Jean could tell Crystal was really excited, as she was
practically vibrating. "Thank you for coming today and for attending
the showing. It means a lot to both Greg and me," Crystal enthused.
"I know success is just beginning for this young man," she gushed
and threw her arms around Greg. Greg's face turned scarlet, but he
hugged her back. Since a line was forming behind them, the
foursome moved on to circulate a bit in the room. After about twenty
minutes the boat started moving away from its docking and out on to
the lake where it would leisurely cruise for about two hours.

John and Jean helped themselves to some hors d'oeuvres and

champagne while Mary Carol and Fred had some white wine. Jean asked Fred, "When do you have to go back to work?"

Fred responded, "I somehow managed to get two days off in a row, so we are staying at the Ameritel until Tuesday morning and then driving back."

Mary Carol joined in while smiling at Fred, "And I took off Monday and Tuesday so we could have a little holiday."

Jean commented, "That is just great. Maybe we can get together for dinner one of these nights," when she felt a subtle nudge on her arm from John, "that is if you two have any free time."

"That would be great," Fred said. How about tonight? That way you two wouldn't have to drive to Coeur d'Alene again and we wouldn't have to drive to Spokane, especially with the cost of gas today."

With that comment John and Fred seemed to suddenly be off in a male bonding world as they discussed ways to get better mileage out of their perspective vehicles. Jean and Mary Carol just smiled at each other and decided to visit with some of the other people who had joined them in the salon. There seemed to be almost fifty people mingling, drinking, snacking, and definitely talking a mile a minute.

After about an hour, Jean and John decided to go up on top to sit in the sun for a while. They found a nice location not too far from where Willy's wife, Margie, had staked herself out. She had all her tanning supplies as well as a soda pop spread out on the little table by her, and she seemed to be sound asleep.

John and Jean spent the next half hour socializing with those who would wander by, enjoying the scenery, and most importantly, enjoying each other. John commented, "Boy, that trip certainly went fast. It seems we will be back at the dock in about ten or fifteen minutes. We should do this more often; I certainly have enjoyed it!" He gave Jean that big smile that made her knees go wobbly and made her toes tingle.

"I have, too. Let's make it a date," Jean laughed and squeezed his hand.

She noticed that Willy had come up to wake up Margie.

As Jean started to say something more to John, she heard Willy call out, "Somebody help me; I can't get Margie to wake up!"

John got up from where he had been sitting with Jean and went to Willy and Margie. Jean saw him shake Margie, at first gently and then quite hard. Jean had a funny feeling and got up to join them. "What's going on?" she inquired.

John replied, "I don't know, but we can't seem to awaken Margie. She has a strong pulse but is unresponsive. Would you go downstairs and ask one of the employees if a doctor is on board?"

Jean rushed downstairs, talked to a steward, and then rushed back to the top deck. She panted," There is no doctor on board, but they have called for paramedics and an ambulance to meet us as soon as we dock. Is there anything else I can do?"

"No, just try to keep Willy calm. I am going to try to keep people downstairs," John answered. Just then they could hear sirens wailing coming down Sherman Avenue towards Independence Point. "I'll try to keep people calm downstairs, also."

Jean knelt down next to Willy, who seemed on the verge of hysterical tears. She was glad to see Crystal come up the stairs, hoping she would be able to keep her son calm, cool, and collected as long as necessary. Jean was surprised to see Max following behind her. Jean realized she hadn't even visited with him, much less seen him on board.

Jean explained, "We can't seem to wake up Margie." Both Max and Crystal seemed shocked and unable to move; they just stood there staring at the comatose body. Just as the Mishanock was pulling up to the shore, Jean turned her head and could see the flashing red lights and men rushing toward the boat.

As Jean turned back, she noticed Max had moved toward the table where all off Margie's tanning materials were resting. He reached down for the bottle of tanning lotion, picked it up, and mumbled, "How could this be happening again?" He then looked at Crystal, threw the bottle at her, and exclaimed, "How could this be happening again?"

Chapter 28
Is This a True Confession?

Crystal looked at Max with a mixture of fear and then anger in her eyes and said in a low voice through clenched teeth, "Don't act like an idiot, you idiot! Keep your voice down and stay cool, for God's sake!" She picked up the bottle Max had thrown at her and handed it back to Max, then grabbed his arm and tried to steer him away from Margie and Willy as the boat bumped against the dock.

Max jerked his arm from Crystal's grasp and in a stage whisper spat out, "You're right; I am an idiot! I was a fool for doing what I did for you thinking it was all for love, and now I can see that the only one you could possibly care about is yourself! You might be beautiful on the outside, Crystal, but inside you are ugly, and sooner or later little Greggy boy is going to find that out, too. And if I have anything to do with it, it will be damned soon!"

Just then the paramedics appeared on the upper deck and, with John leading the way, hurried over to where Margie was lying on the lounge chair. As they began lifting Margie's unconscious form from the lounge to a waiting stretcher, Jean stood up quickly and whispered to John what she had overheard of the exchange between Crystal and Max.

John took a step toward Max as Mary Carol and Fred hurried over from the top of the stairs to see what had caused all the commotion.

"Jean! What on earth is going on?" Mary Carol exclaimed. "When John came down to the lower deck alone and started blocking people from going up the stairs, I was scared to death something had happened to you. Thank goodness you're all right!"

John took hold of Fred's arm and pulled him aside, whispered something to him, and together they hurried to Max. Moving as a single unit, each of them took one of Max's arms and swept him away from Crystal and off to a corner of the deck.

"Wh-what on earth?" stammered Mary Carol. Then she watched the paramedics scurry away with Margie strapped to the stretcher. Willy followed close behind them. "Good grief! What happened to Margie?"

Jean's eyes were glued to the corner where John and Fred were trying to calm Max, who was obviously close to hysteria. "She did it! It was all Crystal's fault. Ask her about the sunscreen and what's in it." At that Max covered his face with his hands and moaned, "Oh, God help us all!"

Crystal took Greg's hand and shook her head. "Obviously Max has had too much to drink once again. Greg, let's go back to our suite. I feel a little faint." She tugged on Greg's hand, and, without a glance at anyone else, hurried him to the stairs to the deck below.

Jean watched them leave and quickly stooped to pick up the sunscreen that Margie had been using.

Fred spoke quietly to Max, "Come on, Max, let's take you somewhere for some coffee and quiet conversation so you can get things sorted out in your head, and we can all make some sense of what's happened here this afternoon." He looked questioningly at John.

"Right!" John agreed. "Jean," he hurried over to her, and spoke very softly. "I'll take both you girls back to your place. Then I'll meet Fred and Max at Marie Calendar's. We could very well end up in the Spokane Police Station later on. I'll try to call you and let you know where we are and what's going on, but don't wait up in case we are late. Get yourselves some dinner, and don't worry about us. Just take care of yourself and Mary Carol, and we'll get back together as soon as we can, okay?"

"Um, well, okay, but please be careful. I think you may be needing this," and she handed him the bottle of sunscreen.

John touched her cheek gently and repeated, "Don't worry." Then he walked over to Fred and Max and spoke quietly with them.

Fred nodded his head and steered Max toward the stairs.

Max was practically babbling by now. "She said if we used the odorless DMSO and dissolved the tranquilizers in it, the sunscreen would make him dizzy, and when he fell and drowned it would look like an accident. Poor Bill! But it was the kindest thing to do really. The Alzheimer's would take away all the good qualities of his life. But Crystal!" Max choked on a sob. "I was such a fool to love her! Such a fool!" He would have stumbled down the stairs if Fred hadn't been holding on to him.

Chapter 29
Waiting to Hear and Wondering

"What could be happening now?" Jean wondered as she wandered aimlessly from room to room with Mrs. Robinson following at her heels. "Why didn't someone call and fill us in? It was the least John could do," she reasoned. She had a panoply of unanswered questions that needed answering.

"For heaven's sake, it is already Monday morning, and I have heard absolutely nothing from John since he dropped us off yesterday afternoon," she mumbled disgustedly to herself. Mrs. Robinson seemed to be pacing with Jean, offering her advice and sympathy with meaningful meows. She and Mary Carol had waited for John and Fred to come back until well after midnight and then had given up and gone to bed. When she had gotten up just after 3:00 A.M. to go to the bathroom (ah yes, the delights of getting older), she had seen Fred's and John's cars in John's driveway next door and the lights on. But when she arose a little after 7:00 this morning, both cars were gone again.

Trying to keep herself occupied this morning, she had already gone through her closet, taking out the summer clothes and replacing them with her autumn and winter things. "What else can I do to keep myself busy?" she wondered. It was almost time for the news on

KREM. She liked the noon news because her former Coeur d'Alene High School student Katie Baker (she could never remember her married name) was the weather person, and she was such a delight! As she walked toward the TV, she wondered when Mary Carol would get back from Coeur d'Alene. She had taken Jean's car and had gone over to gather their things and check out of the motel. "Hmmmm, not a very romantic getaway for Mary Carol and Fred," Jean sighed. She flipped on the TV, hoping to be diverted. To her surprise, Dawn Pickens came on the screen saying there was breaking news from the Spokane International Airport. Shannon Sims was reporting with the story. She said that she and a crew had come to the airport to film the departure of Crystal Pemberton and Greg Applebee on a European tour of the western states to promote Greg's paintings. The tour was supported by the Northwestern Artists Foundation. Just as Crystal Pemberton had been explaining the purpose of the tour, she had been interrupted as policemen appeared and arrested her for the murder of her husband Bill Pemberton.

Shannon explained," Here's what happened."

The screen segued to a very attractive woman in an ivory silk suit talking about what an incredible talent Greg Applebee was. The camera swung to an attractive, young man next to her. He was blushing but smiling as the striking woman continued, "We are embarking on what we hope will be the making of this fine young artist."

Suddenly a group of men, some wearing police uniforms and some in plain clothes, surrounded the woman.

One of the men, an older man with gray hair and a heavy build, stepped closer to her and said, " I am Detective Philip Jonz of the Spokane Police Department. In conjunction with the Montana State Patrol, Crystal Pemberton, I must arrest you as a suspect for the murder of your husband, Bill Pemberton." He reached for her arms with handcuffs extended.

The woman twisted away and looked as though she were ready to flee. The young man with her had paled and was saying, "No, no, nooooooo!"

The woman started to shriek as the detective grabbed her arms and put the handcuffs on. Suddenly she stopped and looked directly at the cameras. She stated very calmly, almost dramatically, "This is a serious mistake which you will regret as soon as I get hold of my attorney, James Kilbourne. My husband died from drowning; it was an accident! I was nowhere near the scene. In fact, I was at home in Missoula many miles away! I can prove it! You will regret this!"

The police had to drag the struggling woman away. Shannon Sims said, "Back to you, Dawn."

Dawn Pickens said, "Be sure to check with us at 5:00 and 6:00 this evening for more news concerning the arrest of Crystal Pemberton for the murder of her husband."

Jean sat down hard with a thump.

Mrs. Robinson jumped into her lap and with a very smug look, settled in for a nap.

Jean could not believe it! Crystal had been arrested for Bill's murder. It certainly explained some of the things Max had been muttering as Fred led him off the Mishanock. She knew that Fred, John, and the other men working the case must have established some pretty strong evidence to go this far.

"Well, as soon as he gets home, John had better have a thorough explanation for all that has transpired!" Jean thought vehemently.

She heard a car in her driveway and rushed to the kitchen window to see who it was. As Mary Carol came through the back door, Jean exclaimed, "Mary Carol, you will not believe what has happened!"

Chapter 30
Resolution

Pacing anxiously from the front window to the kitchen and back with Mrs. Robinson hurrying to keep up, it was all Jean could do to keep from screaming aloud. Instead she opted to converse with Mrs. Robinson and Mary Carol. "Well, how little we really know our friends. Crystal, the sleek and sophisticated art connoisseur, turns out to be implicated in her husband's murder. Poisonous beauty at its very best, methinks. Her promising young artist friend is undoubtedly involved too. Where oh where does that leave Max, to say nothing of Willy and Margie? I do hope she is all right. Did Crystal even imagine the consequences of her horrific plot? Losing her husband might have been one thing, but for heaven's sake she could have lost her son and Margie, too. Whoever said, 'Something evil this way comes,' certainly hit the nail on the head. Seems to me we could certainly add…it comes and comes and comes." Mrs. Robinson meowed in agreement.

Mary Carol could only listen and shake her head in amazement. "You might be perplexed, but I am totally thunderstruck. I live next door to the woman and went through the whole death thing with Bill. Never a clue did I have."

As she nervously trod once more through the dining room, Jean heard a car door slam in John's driveway. By the time she and Mary Carol reached the front door, John and Fred were walking wearily up the front steps.

John's wan face somehow produced a smile for her and he almost pleaded, "How about coffee first, conversation second, Jean Queen?"

"Gracious goodness, guys, it's almost noon. Have you had any breakfast either?"

"Can't say that we have, Jean," Fred replied. "Police headquarters' coffee that was probably brewed yesterday is about the only sustenance we've had."

"Well, come into the kitchen, and I'll put on a fresh pot and scramble some eggs. There might even be some homemade cinnamon rolls in the freezer, but I simply don't know how much longer I can wait to hear what happened."

As Jean drew the water and prepared to brew a fresh pot of coffee, John, Mary Carol, and Fred drew themselves up to the kitchen table and began the final chapter of the story that had begun early in the summer with an e-mail pleading for Jean's help in discovering why a marriage of thirty years had gone awry.

"I guess the best way to proceed here is to begin with what happened after the boat cruise on Sunday," Fred started. "Max's confession started the ball rolling and prompted not only his arrest, but a warrant for Crystal's too."

"Indeed, I saw her arrest on TV this morning. It seems like a nightmare, but everyone is wide awake," Jean replied.

"Speaking of wide awake." John interrupted, "how's the coffee doing?"

"Almost done, "Mary Carol smiled. "And the rolls are heating too. Continue somebody, We have a million questions."

John, fueled by the promise of hot coffee and rolls, took over the narrative. "Because the whole affair had taken place in Missoula, Fred called in Sunday night and was granted permission to stay and be a part of the interrogation. He was able to talk to both Crystal and Greg this morning after their arrest."

MURDER IS ONLY SKIN DEEP

"Did Crystal confess?" "Mary Carol inquired hurriedly.

"Yup, she did crack rather quickly," Fred continued. "The pressure of dealing with Bill's Alzheimer's apparently was too much for her, and the solace of Max's company must have provided a preferable alternative. At any rate, they concocted a scheme that must have seemed almost foolproof—drug Bill while he was fishing and make it seem like a tragic accident. Using DMSO plus a potent tranquilizer that the doctor had prescribed for Crystal, the sunscreen became a lethal weapon. DMSO enabled the absorption of the tranquilizer very quickly and undoubtedly caused Bill to become disoriented and confused; he left his wader belt on shore and since he was fishing in some pretty rapid waters, he probably stumbled, and when his waders filled with water, he was unable to recover."

"So, was the wicked witch after her own son as well? How on earth did Willy get his hands on the sunscreen? Good grief, he was almost burned to a crisp and then poor Margie too. Is she all right?" "Jean queried.

"Yes," John responded. "While Fred was in the interrogation room this morning, I made a trip to Kootenai Medical Center and talked to Willy, who reported that Margie recovered consciousness last night and could probably be dismissed this afternoon. He, of course, is devastated about his mother, but after some gentle probing, we began to put together the pieces of the puzzle.

"After Bill's body was recovered, Willy went with Crystal to gather his father's effects—the fishing tackle, the cooler, the clothes he had taken with him. He wanted to keep his dad's fishing gear and took it home with him to Spokane, but the sunscreen he simply put in the medicine cabinet in his old room at his parent's house."

"Well, that explains his dilemma," Jean mused," but how did Margie get it?"

"The best explanation for that is that he simply packed it in his dop kit when he came home after that incident in Missoula and has had no occasion to use it until the boat cruise when he gave it to Margie." John replied.

"No offense, Fred, but it certainly seems the Missoula police investigation was remiss in this whole thing. Why, oh, why was there no toxicology screen?" Jean questioned.

"There is no sense in worrying about the past, Jean. We know it was sloppy medical work as well as a case of whom you know and not what you know. Crystal and Manheim were friends, and he opted out of careful procedures to help out a friend in crisis mode." Fred returned as gently as he could.

"Plus, my dear, the plot thickens, "John went on. "Surely, the coffee is ready, and the rolls must be piping hot by now."

"Oh, yes, the coffee is ready. John why don't you pour us all a cup and I'll put the finishing touches on the eggs and get the rolls out of the oven."

After everyone was served and had time for a second breath, Jean could bear it no longer. "Ok, John, how do we get any thicker than murder?" she questioned.

"You do remember your nocturnal phone calls, don't you?" John returned.

"Yes, of course, I do," Jean responded. "What's the connection?"

"In the process of interrogating Greg Applebee," Fred went on, "he came clean about the incident when the green car almost ran you down. He was clearly under the spell of Crystal and wanted to scare you away from any further investigation."

"Hmmm," Jean bristled. "Little did he know that scare tactics would only make me more determined! What's to become of him for the part he played in all of this?"

"It will be up to you to press charges, Jean," John replied. "I frankly think you should. Artistic promise be damned, we must all face up to the consequences of our acts."

"I suppose I agree, even though there was no real physical harm none, other than a few bruises,." Jean ruminated. "Nonetheless, you certainly can't run over everyone in life who gets in your way, now can you?

"And what of Max? How I dread telling Beth about this mess. She will be devastated to know that her husband of so many years was not only a conniving adulterer, but a murderer as well."

"Seems to me that what I saw of Beth when she was here, "John interrupted, "showed that she is made of pretty stern stuff. I'm sure she'll gather her wits about her and count herself lucky that the old boy is out from under her roof."

"You could be right, John, "Jean returned, "and I guess that all of us have some lucky stars to count. The bitter and the sweet always balance out some way, don't they?"

Mrs. Robinson, who had been sitting nearby, looked up and meowed as if she agreed.

John smiled tiredly as he finished his coffee and glanced at Mrs. Robinson and then Jean. "Yes, my sweets, they do."

Fred seemed to study the three people in front of him and smiled as well before he replied. "In fact, this whole affair has left four of us with some sweetness to be thankful for. Speaking of which, Jean, could I use your phone? I need to make a call to Missoula, and then we have to make some plans to go home," and Fred gave Mary Carol a weary, but very warm smile.

Printed in the United States
66908LVS00002B/154-159